HERE FOR A GOOD TIME

KIM SPENCER

Text copyright © 2026 by Kim Spencer
Cover art copyright © 2026 by Jazz Aline

Swift Water Books, an imprint of Tundra Book Group, a division of Penguin Random House Canada Ltd., 320 Front Street West, Suite 1400, Toronto, Ontario, M5V 3B6, Canada
penguinrandomhouse.ca

Published simultaneously in the United States of America by Tundra Books of Northern New York, an imprint of Tundra Book Group, a division of Penguin Random House Canada Ltd., P.O. Box 2040, Plattsburgh, NY 12901, USA

Swift Water Books and colophon are trademarks of Penguin Random House Canada Ltd.

All rights reserved. No part of this book may be reproduced, scanned, transmitted, or distributed in any form or by any electronic or mechanical means, including information storage and retrieval systems, without permission in writing from the publisher, except by a reviewer, who may quote brief passages in a review. No part of this book may be used or reproduced in any manner for the purpose of training artificial intelligence technologies or systems.

The authorized representative in the EU for product safety and compliance is Penguin Random House Ireland, Morrison Chambers, 32 Nassau Street, Dublin D02 YH68, Ireland, https://eu-contact.penguin.ie

Publisher's note: This book is a work of fiction. Names, characters, places and incidents either are the product of the author's imagination or are used fictitiously, and any resemblance to actual persons living or dead, events, or locales is entirely coincidental.

Library and Archives Canada Cataloguing in Publication

Title: Here for a good time / Kim Spencer.
Names: Spencer, Kim, author.
Identifiers: Canadiana (print) 2025018883X | Canadiana (ebook) 2025019080X | ISBN 9781774887806 (hardcover) | ISBN 9781774887813 (EPUB)
Subjects: LCGFT: Novels.
Classification: LCC PS8637.P4735 H47 2026 | DDC jC813/.6—dc23

Library of Congress Control Number: 2025937519

Editorial Director, Swift Water Books: David A. Robertson
Edited by Lynne Missen
Designed by Sophie Paas-Lang
Production edited by Bharti Bedi
Typeset by Terra Page
The text was set in Bembo.

Raise a Little Hell - Trooper - Copyright Ramon McGuire and Brian Smith; We're Here for a Good Time (Not a Long Time) - Trooper - Copyright Ramon McGuire and Brian Smith; Santa Maria - Trooper - Copyright Ramon McGuire and Brian Smith; Baby Woncha Please Come Home - Trooper - Copyright Ramon McGuire and Brian Smith

Printed in Canada

1 2 3 4 5   30 29 28 27 26

Dear Reader,

This novel is a reflection of the strength and resilience of a fictionalized Indigenous community in the face of generational trauma. The focus is on strong, loving family and friendship ties. However, there is content that may be triggering, including mentions of residential school trauma, past sexual assault and suicide.

Please note I use outdated language throughout as this is a work of historical fiction set in the nineties.

Kim

For RG

House Party

I wake to the sound of a low rhythmic beat. I glance at the clock and groan. I'm in no mood. I climb out of bed, reach for a hoodie, and pull it over my shoulders. As I make my way down the stairs, Trooper's hit song starts playing again.

"Raise a little hell of your own," a drunken man slurs. The guy can barely raise his head.

"*Jesus Christ, Dad*," I say as I walk into the living room. "Tell your damn friends to leave."

Dad's party must have started after the bar closed. A few stragglers are still going at 6 a.m. It's a sad sight. I had fallen asleep with my headphones on, but still, I can't believe I slept through all the noise.

"*Morgan*, relax. I'm catching up with some friends." Dad grumbles. My dad can handle his booze, for the most part. He looks more tired than drunk.

I turn on my heel and head back upstairs, slamming my bedroom door and locking it. My dad's been bringing parties home since I was a kid. Even when my mom was still here, they'd have friends over. It didn't usually bother me — that's not exactly true, because it *did*. I just didn't know any other way. Isn't that what most parents do?

When I was younger, I'd bartend and play DJ. I'd keep my eye on things, too, making sure no funny business went on. Speaking up with authority if I didn't like something. Dad always backed me, of course. "She's the boss," he'd reply with shrugged shoulders.

My mother took off on us when I was ten. So I *am* the boss. I do most of the organizing and cleaning. And I'm always on Dad's case about something, especially when he blows so much money at the bar.

Dad's a commercial fisherman. He owns his own gillnetter and license. He makes our mortgage and truck payments on time. Keeps up with the maintenance on his boat and our house. He's definitely a hardworking man. He's also a kind, generous, and loving father. Other than the occasional house party, things are usually pretty tame at home. Boring even.

"Time to go. Call yourselves a cab," I hear Dad say.

I put my headphones back on to drown them out. I am not in the mood to hear my own thoughts, let alone drunks carrying on.

My mother lives in Vancouver now. She's an alcoholic on skid row. At least that's the last I'd heard. I try not to think about her. And I don't let my father reminisce about her either. He used to say things like, "Your mom made the best eets'm anaay."

She did make the best frybread.

Or "Your mom used to love to harvest seafood."

Or "She used to knit me the best wool toques for fishing."

I didn't want to hear it. Did he think I didn't remember her? Didn't remember the way she'd hum as she cooked tasty meals? Her gentle, soothing voice? How immaculately clean she kept our house? The pride she took in ironing Dad's button-up shirts?

He's a fisherman, for crying out loud. Why would he need his shirts ironed?

But she liked him to look sharp when they went out. The generous "highliner" he is, always picking up the tab.

It makes me sad that he keeps a picture of her on his dresser. She's strikingly beautiful in it, with her brown sun-kissed skin, high cheekbones, and wide smile. She's standing at the stove holding up a live crab, an oversized sweatshirt hanging from her slim frame, her eyes beaming.

Dad is handsome and fairer-skinned — a Native mother and white father. He's also charismatic and funny as hell. The life of the party. A nice complement to my mother's shy, reserved demeanor. Together, they had made quite the pair, the kind of couple people gravitated toward. Hence the wide network of friends and house parties.

I guess I fell back asleep. When I wake up, I look at the clock and see it is noon.

THE CARNIVAL

It's nearing the end of summer. The carnival is in town this weekend and a group of my friends decide to go together. My dad gave me extra money, obviously feeling guilty after his late-night party incident. We find a "runner" to get us booze. It's never a problem in this town. There's always someone willing to buy alcohol for underage teens — especially if you tell them they can keep the change.

We get a couple of two-liters of California Coolers, then make our way to the field beside the Civic Centre. There's a secluded dugout we can drink them in without getting caught. My best friend Skye and I like the orange flavor the best. We pass it back and forth, drinking from the bottle. The concept of cups never enters our minds. We drink half and save the rest for later.

We make our way to the carnival feeling tipsy. And a bit giddy. Colorful lights illuminate the dark night. Music blares from each ride as we walk past. Greasy-looking white guys are pushing games. "Step right up and win your prize."

Skye and I put our money together and buy a packet of tickets. The first ride we go on is the Spider. Skye flirts with the operator so he'll let us stay on longer. "Can you give us a spin?" She smiles sweetly. He does. Of course he does. Skye is striking; she's pale-skinned with raven-black hair and has wide hazel eyes. A Native mom and a Norwegian father.

The ride is in full motion and a Nazareth song is playing. Skye and I are laughing from all the whirling. We eventually tire of holding our heads up and lean back, resting our necks on the seat and staring up at the night sky. Smiles on our faces, lost in the music and our wine cooler buzz.

We also go on the Zipper, which I hate. Why would anyone want to get flipped around like that? With just enough tickets left for one last ride, I pick something more my pace — the Ferris wheel.

As the ride is loading, we end up stopped at the top. It's a great view of all the lights, striped tent tops, and people milling about. We spot the others at the corn dog stand. A cute Native guy is standing with them. His name is Nate Jones. I've never met him, but I've seen him around.

"Do you know that guy standing there?" I ask.

Skye squints her eyes. "Is that Nate?" Then starts yelling out, "Hey!" Waving at them.

"Guys!" we both yell.

They don't hear us.

After the ride, we rejoin our group. Nate is no longer with them, but I'm glad we're all together. Carnival guys have been catcalling Skye, and she always responds, chatting with them. She thinks she's being cheeky. I say stupid. I guess no one's told her to be cautious of transient carnival guys, although it should be obvious. God knows, my nana has instilled the fear in me. She's always warning me of what "could" happen. She's a worrier like that. I don't know why — our little town seems safe enough. Well, except for that young Native woman who died last summer. Hikers found a body just off the highway outside of town. She wasn't from around here, so my family didn't know her. It was so sad and scary. Especially since they still don't know who did it.

KEEP IT

I once had a job waitressing at Nick's pizza parlor. I guess it was hardly a *job*, as I only worked one night. It was more like filling in for Skye. It's the only restaurant in town open until 3 a.m.

Nick is the Greek owner and chef who lives in an apartment above the restaurant. He's a large, disheveled-looking man who wears his shirt unbuttoned low. Too low for a chef. And looks like he should wash his hands more often, *especially for a chef.* He can usually be found smoking a cigarette at the side door just off the kitchen.

Nick's is located across the street from our main bar district. After the bars close, people spill into the street, lingering in a crowd. It's almost a party in itself. It even has its own name: "bar crowd." People look for a house party, try to hail a taxi, or even get into a fistfight. A few revelers head over to the run-down pizza parlor for late-night eats.

I did well for a first-timer. I only messed up one order, which inadvertently turned into two. After digging into his meal, a customer said, "I ordered a vegetarian lasagna." I was surprised the drunken man could tell the difference. As I was returning to the kitchen with his *not* vegetarian dish, a Native guy at another table said, "This lasagna is tasteless." *Ah, found the vegetarian one!* Nick glared at me when I told him I needed two more dishes.

I approached another table to take an order. "We're Here for a Good Time" by Trooper came on the jukebox. The table started singing along. They were fishermen, not from around here. I decided to share a bit of Rupert's trivia with them: "Did you know this song was written about Prince Rupert?"

"Get outta here, really?" a white lady slurred. Then added, "That's awesome," and started singing even harder, *"And the sun is shinin' in this rainy city."*

She emphasized the rainy part.

"It's a little-known fact," I added.

Prince Rupert, British Columbia, is an infamous party town. Trooper is considered "Canada's Party Band." The match makes perfect sense. People flock to town for the summer to fish; they make a ton of money, have a good time, and then leave. Sometimes, they take or leave more than they bargained for. It's 1990, and even though that old hit came out over ten years ago, it's still played regularly on the radio, at bars, and at house parties. Native households especially.

At the end of the night, a server cleared her table after a group of fishermen left. She ran out the door after one of them, extending her hand out toward him and said, "Hey, you dropped your money."

I was clearing a table near the door. I overheard the fisherman reply, "Keep it."

"It's a thousand-dollar bill," the server replied. He paused and considered her words. "Keep it." He waved his hand dismissively and climbed into the back of a taxi.

We're here for a good time
Not a long time

WHAT WOULD JACKIE COLLINS DO?

Skye recently taught me how to shoplift. We had been walking in Zellers when I saw a glass vase. "That's cute," I'd said, picking it up and admiring it.

"You like it; you should have it," she had replied.

I glanced at her.

"Take it," Skye said.

My eyes widened. I glanced around before carefully sliding it up my sleeve. Once I got outside and realized I hadn't been caught, I held it up, practically announcing *I stole this!* Staring at it in awe.

That's how I discovered Jackie Collins. I was grocery shopping at Safeway with my dad and saw a paperback of *Hollywood Wives* and discreetly slid it into my bag. I don't know why I did it. If I'd tossed the book in our buggy, my dad wouldn't have noticed or questioned it. But it was the thrill of it. I felt cool stealing. Like Skye.

I read the book in no time. I couldn't put it down. Once I finished it, I read every other book of hers I could get my sticky little hands on. When faced with decisions, I started asking myself: *What would Jackie do?* She would have stolen the book, of course.

My favorite series is the one featuring the Santangelo family. Especially Lucky. Lucky Santangelo is a smart, gorgeous, headstrong woman. An absolute powerhouse. Sure, the books are pretty raunchy — "smut," Skye calls them. But I skim past those parts. At least that's what I tell myself. I enjoy the far-flung corners of the world the books take me to: sipping red wine along the Mediterranean; flying the Concorde from London to New York. But for the most part, I love the gangsters, like Lucky's father, Gino Santangelo. I read the books again and again. Lose myself in the world of the Santangelos. Small-town living is just that — small. Jackie Collins's books open a world of "other" for me. *There's life beyond Rupert? Who knew!*

SCHOOL

My mom left us when I was in fifth grade. That's when I first started missing school. It was like she had died — she was suddenly gone and no one talked about it. Dad must have tried to explain, but I don't remember. Not that it would have made a difference. I was devastated. My whole world changed. I became quiet and withdrawn. Developed constant tummy aches.

I had been a strong student before she left. After, I started to complain that I was sick, and my dad would let me stay home, barely putting up an argument. After a few years of carrying on that way, it was no surprise that high school was a challenge for me. I couldn't keep up or find a place for myself, and not just academically either. In Prince Rupert, we have a high school that goes from eighth to tenth grade, and then a senior high school for eleventh and twelfth grades. I met Skye when I was in eighth grade, and she was in tenth. We ended up skipping class together and quickly became best friends. She was so easygoing and carefree. I'd never met anyone like her.

When I got my report card at the end of the year, I couldn't believe they'd moved me on to ninth grade. F's and all! I barely attended classes for the ninth grade either. Then we went to Hawaii for Christmas. Dad, Nana, Grandpa, and me. We'd vacationed there many times. Even when my mom was around, we'd go.

We rented a condo and stayed for two months. It had been a good season for sockeye salmon. There's nothing quite like the feeling and smell when you get off the airplane in Honolulu. The scents of orchards and fragrant plumerias, the warm trade winds, and Hawaiian music playing — the *Aloha spirit*. Other Native fishermen were vacationing with their families, too, people we'd known for years. Native men blended in like they were locals. Deep tans and Aloha shirts. The women always wore a fresh lei or put a flower behind their ears when going out.

Our condo was within walking distance of the beach, nothing fancy, but a comfortable space filled with rattan furniture, mother-of-pearl lampshades, and teak bowls.

Nana loves all that stuff. We went to a hula show, and Dad got called onto the stage. I'd never seen him move his hips like that before. It was hilarious. I'm sure the rum helped. We all had a good laugh and got pictures. Dad and Grandpa might have drank a mai tai too many. Not Nana though; she nurses her drinks. Ever composed, Nana. We also shopped at the International Market for souvenirs and took a family photo with parrots — Aloha shirts and dresses on, our tanned skin, and happy faces. Grandpa and Dad went on a marlin sportfishing charter, too. It was expensive, but it looked to be a blast from the pictures. We happily spent most of our holiday swimming and eating warm pineapple on the beach.

When we finally returned home, I didn't bother going back to school. What was the point? Dad pressured me for a while and told me to at least look into correspondence, but I never got around to it.

ALTERNATE SCHOOL

It is now September, and technically, I should be starting tenth grade. Skye was kicked out ages ago. She'd registered at Kaien Island Alternate School and told me to do the same. Prince Rupert is located on Kaien Island. A short bridge connects us to the mainland, so a lot of businesses in town are named after it. If we're out of town and spot a car with a Kaien Island Ford sticker, we say, "Hey, Rupert people!"

The school is a two-story building located off the field of PRSS, Prince Rupert Senior Secondary. It's the size of a large house. Skye says the school has around thirty students. I already know and hang out with a few of them, so I feel comfortable entering the building.

Bryan, the head instructor, is a slight man with graying hair, a gray mustache and metal-framed glasses. He seems intense but in a curious way.

"You live at home with your parents?" he asks.

"With my dad, but he's fishing." I can see the wheels turning. White adults tend to feel sorry for me, especially if they know my mom left. They probably think I mind being left alone all the time. (I don't.)

After making small talk, Bryan takes me for a short tour. There's the main room with an adjoining kitchen. Across the hall is a separate lounge with two couches, a pool table, and a foosball table! Bryan quickly states, "The rules are strictly enforced around this room. Games can only be played at recess, lunch, or after school." He holds my gaze hostage as he says it, making sure I understand.

I nod, to let him know I am following.

Skye has claimed a small back room for herself. She said no one else seemed to sit there. The downstairs area has an open space, and a stereo is playing music low. There's one computer. Bryan says something about it having a dial-up modem. I have no idea what he's talking about.

Students are sitting at tables or cubicles working, a mixture of Native students and a few white kids.

We end the tour back in his office. It takes some time to convince Bryan that I belong at Alternate School. He initially told me I wasn't a good candidate. Maybe because

I know how to carry a conversation and make eye contact when I speak. Interacting with adults is nothing for me. I'm an only child. I explain to Bryan that I hadn't attended school since last December, and that I'd been struggling for years before that. "Especially after my mother left us," I throw in for good measure. To seal the deal.

He stares me in the eye. Processing what I'd said. Then he hands me paperwork to fill out. When we are done, he says, "We're happy to have you, Morgan. You'll find Alternate School to be a supportive place."

NATE

It's the beginning of October when *he* shows up: Nate Jones, the cute guy from the corn dog stand. He seems familiar and friendly with students here, yet at the same time, he looks like he doesn't belong. He's medium height, fair-skinned with a stocky build. He's wearing a navy cable-knit sweater and dark blue jeans. At first glance, you might not guess he's Native. Well, a white person might not. Natives recognize Natives. Even if you're in an unfamiliar place. You know.

I'm sitting downstairs, working on an assignment with a schoolmate. Nate is sitting close by. I do my best to act like I don't notice. At recess, when the teacher goes upstairs, Nate asks, "What are you reading?" I hold my book up for him to read the cover. *Lady Boss*, Jackie Collins's latest novel.

"Ah. What's it about?" Nate questions.

"Gangsters," I reply coolly.

"Oh." Then he asks, "Like the Gambino crime family?"

"Who are they?"

"Italian American gangsters."

I lower my book.

He readily explains the inner workings of the Gambino crime family like he's narrating a documentary. He's talking about the "five families," detailing how the empire is run. I'm familiar with the language from Jackie Collins novels but his recounting fascinates me. He's articulate and confident.

Without missing a beat he moves on to telling me about books he likes to read. *Dickens?* I make the mistake of asking him what the books are about. He starts to provide a summary. He's talking about someone named Pip, and class and identity. We talk like we've known each other forever, even though this is our first conversation. Before we know it, it's lunchtime.

The next time we chat is after Thanksgiving. He'd just come back from Vancouver with his family. He tells me about shopping at Ming Wo in Chinatown and eating at Tsunami Sushi on Robson Street, how sushi trays float around a bar on little boats, and you have to grab the ones you want to eat. I've never even tried sushi before. My dad has. He loves the stuff. Then Nate says he shopped at The Body Shop, and that he bought his girlfriend stuff there. *He has a girlfriend!* We continue talking, and talking, *friends*, talking.

THEY'RE JUST AS BAD

I come home from school to find Dad dancing while he's cooking. He's really gettin' down. He does this often, especially when he's in a good mood. I kick my shoes off at the door and ask, "*What* are you listening to?" I chuckle.

"It's ska."

"It's what, now?" I walk to the counter, grab a washed grape tomato, and pop it in my mouth.

"It's like reggae; it's a new album I picked up this morning at Teddy's."

My dad is a serious vinyl record collector. I'm sure he's kept Teddy's Records in business all these years. Most recently, he's started buying CDs. They are the latest in technology. They say they're damn near indestructible, with perfect sound. And they'll be around a long, long time. I'm used to him introducing me to cool music, like

Robbie Robertson, Leonard Cohen, and Roberta Flack.

"Sounds groovy," I say and head upstairs to my room.

Dad's making pasta with scallops for dinner. He's a good cook and likes trying new things. Most fishermen can cook. You have to. Women are rarely on the boat. Plus, Nana's a great cook — he's grown up around good food. I, however, did not inherit that gene. I cannot cook. Seriously, I burn *water*.

We mostly eat seafood. As coastal Natives, we live off the sea. Our backyard. Sockeye, spring salmon, halibut, oolichans, prawns, crab — you name it, we got it. Heck, even urchins! We're lucky.

When Dad and I sit down for dinner, he starts right in telling me the latest. Fishermen always know the latest. He said a buddy of his bought a house that a Department of Fisheries officer had owned. "And get this: It has a state-of-the-art smokehouse in the backyard!"

I stop twirling the noodles with my fork. "That smells fishy."

"Right? For an officer whose job is seizing fish from Native people. They're just as bad as the police."

TROOPER CONCERT

Trooper is in town! *Trooper!* In *Prince Rupert*. I can hardly believe it. I'm currently obsessed with the song "Boy with a Beat." Actually, the entire album is good. I bought the cassette when it first came out. *Yes, bought.* You can't steal anything from East Wind Emporium. They're all eagle eyes when you shop there. They don't even try to hide it either.

Trooper is going to be playing at Bogey's nightclub, and you have to be nineteen to get in. Skye and I have been scheming ways to get fake IDs. The only place you can get a fake ID is Vancouver — even then, it's not a guarantee. Bouncers can spot fakes a mile away. Skye's older sister Cheryl comes up with an ingenious idea: borrow Indian status cards, put our pictures over the top, and get a self-sealing laminating kit. She says to ask someone who isn't a Bogey's regular. Someone the bouncer,

Ray, won't recognize. And she says the age has to be nineteen, because there is no way we can pass for any older. We rack our brains, and eventually, come up with two prospects. We beg to borrow their cards, assure them we won't lose them, and promise to return the cards right after. It takes some convincing, but they finally agree.

We swipe laminating packs from the stationary store. Then comb through our photo albums, looking for pictures. At last, we stare at our counterfeit cards. They don't look bad. They don't look good either. Much too bulky for ID. Identification that's been twice laminated.

We buy the tickets with money my dad gives me. On the night of the concert, Skye and I decide to get ready at Cheryl's. We grab a six-pack of Pilsner and head over. We figure we can all go together. It will be less obvious that we are underage. Skye has chosen a short fuchsia jersey dress and a black cropped leather jacket. She looks stunning. Jaw-dropping. I wear a short black dress with a cream blazer, my trusty gold hoop earrings and black pumps complete the outfit — I can totally pass for nineteen!

Cheryl ditches us at the last minute and gets a friend to pick her up. She said it'll be too embarrassing if we don't get in. Skye is pissed with her.

We take a cab to the club and make our way toward the entrance. Those few beers helped ease our nerves. Good ol' liquid courage.

Skye enters ahead of me — that's our first mistake. I'm wearing a blazer. *Hello, old person.* I should have gone first.

"ID, both of you," the bouncer, who I assume is Ray, asks.

We dig into our purses for our status cards. They're government-issued ID cards — why wouldn't he accept them?

The bouncer is an Asian man with a shaved head, wearing a lightweight baseball jacket as he casually leans against a rail at the top of the staircase. We can hear Trooper playing "Workin' Like a Dog." The beat of the live drums sends tingles up my spine — the energy is exhilarating. I want to push past him and run down the stairs.

We hand him the cards. He barely glances at our faces, then points his flashlight at our ID and says, "Whose pictures are underneath the lamination?"

He doesn't wait for a reply. He hands them back, and says, "Get outta here. Quit wasting my time."

Skye and I nearly stumble over each other, scrambling to get out the door. As soon as we exit, we burst into nervous laughter.

"Thanks for nothing, *Ray!*" Skye hollers over her shoulder.

We walk to the end of the block, still giggling, then turn the corner by the Rupert Hotel. "I totally thought we would get in!" I make a pouty face.

"We were this close," Skye says, holding up her thumb and index finger.

I make another sad face, sharing my total disappointment. "What should we do with our tickets?"

"Let's hang out and see if we can sell them," Skye answers, her eyes already scanning the area.

"Are we ticket scalpers now? Do you think this is Vancouver?"

She ignores me.

"Hey, you guys need tickets for the concert?" Skye asks passersby. "Fifty bucks for two." She says it like she's a natural. A pro. I find it embarrassing. She's already onto the next person. "Last chance for tickets — the concert's sold out."

We end up selling them for thirty dollars. Enough to buy beer and grab a cab to a house party.

ANNIVERSARY CELEBRATION

It's my grandparents' thirty-fifth anniversary, and we're having a party at the Elks Hall tonight. Nana stops by this afternoon to drop off a shopping bag for Dad. New clothes for the party. She knows he would never shop for dress clothes on his own. She's really into appearances — he's not.

They live on Overlook Street; we're nearby on Ambrose, so Nana drops by often. Their house has an incredible view of the harbor. Grandpa does well as a commercial fisherman. He owns a herring seiner and a couple of licenses. Nana loves to brag about Grandpa's fishing prowess. She'll say things like, "The fish follow him around!" Or "The fish practically jump into his net!" When Nana was younger, she used to fish with Grandpa, and he'd say, "Nana has eyes like a hawk. She's always the first to spot fish." Or "She's my best spotter girl." You can tell she loves it when he says stuff like that, even though she tries not to show it. They're adorable.

"What are you wearing for tonight, Morgie?"

She's standing in the doorway of my bedroom. Her eyes scan the room, seeing if it is tidy. *Her* standard of tidy. Dad calls her QC behind her back. She's quality control, all right. Only thing she's missing is a white glove.

I don't usually fuss about what I wear. "I'm heading to Zellers in a bit to grab something," I mumble.

"My one and only granddaughter will *not* get a dress from there!" You'd think I had said the thrift store by Nan's response.

"Come on, we are going to Mantique," she enthusiastically replies. Then adds, "Isn't that where you young kids shop these days?"

I said Zellers because I'd gotten into the habit of stealing from there with Skye. It's more like *a bad habit* — what if we were caught? I felt ashamed at the very thought. I was chatting with Nate the other day when he said, referring to Skye, "Like her family. They're known thieves." He'd said it with such disdain. Like it was the lowest thing.

I make my way through Mantique. A black off-the-shoulder fitted body dress catches my eye. I grab a size small and head to the changing room, take my clothes off, and pull the dress over me. I exit to look in the three-way mirror.

"Look at my granddaughter!" Nana says to the salesgirl. "You don't see a shapely figure like that every day."

Then leans in and whispers to me, *"And those breasts."*

"Nan, stop." I sigh, and stare at my reflection. I'm not used to wearing dresses, but this dress makes me feel sexy — look sexy!

"Who knew you had them, always hiding under sweatshirts." Still staring, she adds, "We should get you a strapless bra, too."

The Elks Hall is packed with Natives from surrounding villages, honoring my grandparents' invitation. Everyone is dressed to the nines: men in suits, the women adorned in their finest garb and gold-carved Native jewelry. I'm grateful Nana bought me my dress. I feel so elegant.

And the seafood spread is delicious: crabs, prawns, and halibut. There's so much food! The speeches are a highlight of the night. Old Native men love to speak from a platform. You don't immediately get where they're going with their story, then BAM! They hit you with something hilarious. And their comedic timing is always spot on.

Seeing my grandparents waltz gets me teary-eyed. Nana looks gorgeous in a black velvet wrap dress with tasteful sequins. She's slim, olive-skinned with wide, bright eyes — still a stunner. And Grandpa is Grandpa, lovable, ever handsome, and jovial.

Older folks sure know how to have a good time. We dance, laugh, and take a ton of pictures. I can't wait to get them developed.

WHY DIDN'T WE MEET BEFORE?

It's the Monday after my grandparents' party. Nate comes to the back room, where I study. Whenever we get the chance to talk at school, we do. As friends, of course. I'm standing, leaning against a table, reading. Skye's still in the lunchroom. We chat about what we're reading, then our foosball averages, which quickly turns into an argument over who's better at pool (I've beaten him in a few games). We sit on top of the table, facing the window that overlooks the field. My black leather backpack is between us. I like that there's a barrier. Some distance.

"Can I look through your bag?" Nate asks.

"Go ahead. There's nothing personal in there."

He starts rummaging through it, pulls out my novel and glances at the cover, puts aside my black eel-skin wallet and then asks, "What's this?"

He's holding a *long, stiff feminine pad*! I'd been short on cash, so I bought the no-name brand. The thing is the size of a two-by-four! Totally archaic-looking, like it needs to be held in place by a belt. I snatch it from him and put it back in my bag. He stares at me. I look away.

"Do you like that Billy Joel song, 'We Didn't Start the Fire'?" I ask.

He immediately goes into the politics of the song and its social relevance.

I was referring to the beat.

"It's a wordy song. It's like he's trying to do rap," he adds.

"Bryan said we could do a social studies assignment on it," I tell him.

"Yeah, you only have to pick a few topics to research. It'd be an easy mark . . ." His words trail off.

We sit quietly, staring straight ahead.

"Why didn't we meet before?" he says, and turns to look at me.

Why didn't we meet before? I can't turn to meet his gaze.

Before Alternate? Before he had a girlfriend?

SHAME

Nate talks about his family a lot. His dad, mom, and older sister, who is off at university. She was just home for the Christmas holidays.

Nate knows my dad from fishing. I have yet to bring up my mom. And, thankfully, he hasn't asked. I feel so much shame over her leaving us, like Dad and I aren't worthy of her. I know that's stupid, though. She didn't leave us for a better place, or another family — she left us for *skid-bloody-row*. I don't know what's more hurtful, her being a skid-row drunk, or that she didn't care enough to stay. And that void, and the ensuing hurt and shame, feel ever-present. Like Jiminy Cricket, on my shoulder.

ALTERNATE SCHOOL RULES

Alternate School is strict about one thing: attendance. If you skip school, you get demerit points against you. You can get them for other reasons, too. Things like acting up or not doing your schoolwork. If you get too many, you're eventually kicked out.

I've always been in the habit of missing school. Like, if I didn't sleep well, or had cramps.

I collect demerits quickly.

Friday afternoon during the break, Skye and I decide to sneak out. We want to head to the mall a bit early. I know I have only one point left. One more strike and I am out. *But who would notice if we left a bit early?*

We get caught.

Bryan calls me into his office the following week. He likes to use fancy words when he speaks, even when there's a simple way of saying something. He tells me we have a *conundrum* on our hands. The teachers vote on individual student cases, taking several factors into consideration. Then he says, "The teachers all voted to expel you. They don't think you're taking your studies seriously."

"I miss school. Big deal. At least I do my work." That's all I can think to say.

"It is a big deal, Morgan." He stares at me. "The sooner you realize that, the better off you'll be."

I say nothing.

"As head of the school, however, I have the final say, and I told them you were staying." He's staring again. Then adds, "I'm not looking to garner praise for myself, but I went to bat for you, Morgan. Don't make me look bad. Prove to them I was right in keeping you."

I thank him and tell him I will. And I mean it. I get up to leave and head for the exit.

"You've received a second chance, Morgan," he calls out. "You're the steward of your life. *You are steering the ship!*"

ALL NATIVE

The All Native Basketball Tournament has been held in Prince Rupert every year since 1959. They say it was formed as a way for Natives to gather safely. For over sixty years, the Canadian federal government had banned Natives from gathering for traditional potlatches. The ban had been lifted, but cultural gatherings were still few and far between.

When teams from surrounding reserves and other community members arrive in town, they are greeted with "Welcome All Native Basketball Players and Fans" signs displayed in storefront windows, and a banner hangs outside of City Hall. Every single hotel room in Prince Rupert is booked for the entire tournament. It's a great boost to the economy, especially during an otherwise slow month of February.

It's been a fun week watching basketball. I go with my dad and grandparents to a few games. We also eat tasty food in the auditorium. Vendors have tables set up selling sweatshirts for their home team, and others sell traditional foods. The clam fritters are always the first thing to sell out. And the xs'waanx (herring eggs).

Eating and visiting with people from different reserves is as important as watching games. You get to know who's who and what nation people are from. Dad knows a lot of people from fishing, so he enjoys visiting with everyone.

There's also an increased police presence during the All Native tournament. They train RCMP officers on riot control here. Send them to the "bar crowd" in Prince Rupert. I guess that's how wild they think Native people are.

It's Friday night, and the tournament semifinals are on. My friend Jess and I make our way to our seats in the stands. She immediately starts whistling and whooping it up, getting other fans around us going. I met Jess last All Native, and even though she's two years older than me, we instantly hit it off. She's a lot of fun, but we don't get to hang out nearly enough. She's always busy with studying and playing basketball. She plays for the Rainmakers, the seniors' basketball team, and she plays in the Junior All Native tournament. Jess also likes to party and have a good time, and she's funny as hell.

After the games, Jess finds out there's a party at a guy named Jason's. We find a runner to get us booze at the beer-and-wine, then we taxi to the party. It's an impressive house in a newer development; new trucks and sports cars are parked out front. Jason's father is a big-time Native fisherman, who owns a roe and kelp license. Dad does well fishing, and we have a nice home, but not like these guys — they're loaded.

The party is already hopping when we walk through the front door. Music is blaring from the Kenwood speakers — the bass is really thumping.

I don't usually hang around with this crowd. Jess, however, announces her arrival with a fist pump and then a *woof-woof-woof* like she's on *Arsenio Hall*. She can be a total tomboy at times. The guys are mostly basketball players, and they join in and egg her on. They're all wearing name-brand clothing — Polo, Mondetta, or FUBU. Their idea of fun seems to be rousing each other with cutting, sarcastic remarks. After listening to a few rounds of zingers, I'm done. I elbow Jess and ask if she wants to look downstairs. She nods, then makes an armpit fart for the guys. Her way of saying goodbye. They all laugh. It's just the reaction she was hoping for.

We make our way down a half-flight of stairs. Girls are gathered in front of a jumbo television screen, doing "the Running Man" to a MuchMusic video. One girl's wearing a white T-shirt with the sleeves rolled, and loose-fitting Levi's, a black leather belt cinched at the waist. Her skin is bronze from a tanning bed — almost orange — and her bangs are teased high.

I watch them for a while, admiring how carefree these Native girls seem. Dancing freestyle with their cute clothes and big hair. I couldn't imagine willingly taking up space like that.

Just then, I feel a palm rest gently on my back and turn around. It's Nate. "I didn't know you were here," he says with a smile.

"Oh hey, yeah, Jess and I just got here." *So, this is the crowd he hangs out with.*

Jess punches him in the arm — "Nate-ster" — and takes off.

Nate and I stand making small talk. I catch myself nervously gulping my drink. He's relaxed, composed, of course, talking about fishing. Then he moves on to what movies are at the theater and complains about there never being anything good in town. I eventually feel myself loosening up. When a love seat opens, Nate motions for us to sit. I can't help but wonder if his girlfriend is here. Then I remember hearing she is white — there are no white people at this party — and push the thought aside.

Before we know it, it's three in the morning. The music has been turned down, and the crowd has thinned. Nate's trying on my carved-silver bracelet. I think they look unusual on guys — I can't tell if they look feminine or confident. I think it also depends on who's wearing them. If you've got money, most definitely confident. Jess starts walking toward us.

"Are you sure you two have *enough* to talk about?"

I smile shyly. A comfortable buzz.

"You've been talking the entire night!" Then she adds, "Come on, Morg, I'm tired."

I'm ready to go as well, so I get up and we say our goodbyes.

In the cab Jess says, "There's gonna be another party here tomorrow." She winks and nudges me. "Maybe Nate will be there."

MONDAY MORNING

Jess's cousins were in town visiting for the tournament, so we ended up at a different party Saturday night. I would have rather gone back to Jason's. However, I did get the scoop on Nate's girlfriend. Jess said they've been going out for *two years*! I didn't realize it was so serious. Not that it matters to me — we're only friends. Although I must admit, it's getting harder and harder to convince myself of that.

When I arrive at school Monday morning, Skye's waiting at the door for me. She drags me to the back room, where we sit. "I tried calling you yesterday — where were you?!"

"I was at my grandparents'. Why?" I reply.

"You aren't going to believe who I was with Saturday night." Her eyes are on fire with excitement.

"Who, and define with?" I say, getting impatient. I haven't even put down my bag.

"Nate, and *with, with*."

I feel it in my throat and then a pang in my stomach. Which I quickly realize is stupid.

"Doesn't he have a girlfriend?" I manage.

"He broke up with her." Her eyes pierce through me. Trying to read my reaction. She knows there's something between Nate and me. "I know you guys are friends. Always talking and stuff." Then adds, "That won't be weird, will it?"

"Why would I care?" I walk away. I've heard enough.

I make my way to the washroom. I've never felt so angry with Skye. Yet at the same time, I feel silly for feeling this way. Nate has a girlfriend. *Had.*

I decide to go and make a hot chocolate. I'm not in the mood for one, but I head to the kitchen anyway. I can't face Skye right now. I stir my drink longer than is necessary. My mind is racing, replaying her words — *with, with.*

I throw myself into my assignment. I get more work done in one morning than I have in a while.

In the late afternoon, I go downstairs to see an instructor. I walk past where Nate sits; he's chatting with another student. When he sees me, he stops talking. He looks almost sheepish. *Guilty.* "Hey," he says, and looks away.

"Hey." I keep walking.

When I'm done speaking with the instructor, I head back upstairs.

Nate says, "We missed you at the party Saturday."

I glance back but say nothing.

JOB PRACTICUM

I'm over being upset with Skye. After all, Nate and I were, oh, um, *nothing*. Besides, she knows what she's done. She has been extra nice to me lately, too. Was it worth it? I wondered. She and Nate aren't an item or anything. They barely say hello when they pass each other.

It's nearing the end of March, and we're going on job practicum placements. I'm surprised employers even want Alternate School students — a bunch of delinquents!

But I'm also glad. I think it'll be fun. You pick two places and work each one for a week.

Skye chooses a video rental store and Reitman's for her placements. I didn't need to see the look on Bryan's face to know they are both missed opportunities.

I choose the hospital because I want to be a practical nurse, but that quickly changes after my practicum. Don't get me wrong — it's necessary, rewarding work. And I did well at my practicum. My review said I was "very mature for my age." But *wiping old people's butts* is no longer a career goal.

The second place I choose is Star of the West Books. My dad and I shop there all the time, but standing on the other side of the counter is different. It's a little piece of Rupert I haven't known. White customers will stack a pile of books on the counter, willingly forking out fifty, sixty, or a hundred dollars. *For books!* It's a luxury I never would have imagined. My dad and I have always bought books, but mainly a paperback or two here and there.

Jason, whose house party I went to with Jess, stops by the store. His mom works at a medical office in the area. We chat briefly until the owner starts glancing over at us. I quickly say goodbye and return to stocking shelves.

The bookstore also gives me a positive review. Bryan reads my feedback aloud to me: "'She handled detailed ISBN book orders with great accuracy.' Both places had such good things to say about you, Morgan." You can tell he is proud of me.

The bookstore offers me a part-time job working

weekends. I don't accept it, though. I can barely get to school, never mind getting up early on weekends. Plus, I can make more money on my dad's boat in one afternoon than working a month at a retail store.

PARSLEY

Prince Rupert's population is pretty much half Native and half white. There are a few other minority races, as well. The two dominant groups mix, for the most part, even date and intermarry. Throughout elementary school, my best friend was white. Drew-Anne. But we gradually went our separate ways when we got to junior high. She gravitated toward white kids, and me, Native girls like Skye.

Skye and I are on our way to the Hotspot, it's our only arcade in town. Mostly, Natives hang out there, and it's a well-known place where people sell drugs.

As we near the front entrance, two popular white girls greet us. They're both stylishly dressed, in all black. They look so city, like they're from Vancouver or something. And the type that probably listens to music like Depeche Mode or New Order. I don't know them, but Skye does.

"Skye! Oh my god, guess what!" the shorter one says.

"Hey, guys, what's up?" Skye says, her eyes toward the entrance, like she's not even listening to them.

"Oh my god, we bought a joint from a guy and smoked it, but seriously, it was parsley! There was, like, no weed in there."

Skye glances at her.

"It was such a rip-off. He filled it with parsley," she adds, eyes glossed over.

"Can you help us get our five bucks back?" the other one pleads.

Skye chuckles. "Sounds like you guys better go smoke some more of that parsley." And she walks past them.

Once inside, I start laughing. "Skye! You totally blew those girls off."

"Who cares — poor, high, rich girls," she says, her eyes scanning the darkened arcade. "I'm sure there's no shortage of five-dollar bills for them."

NDN BEER

Skye and I are at a house party, sitting on a couch. When the seat beside me opens up, a guy I don't know immediately sits down.

"Eee, why are you drinking NDN beer?" he asks.

I glance at the can of Canadian in my hand, then at the bottle of Coors Light in his.

"You should be drinking Coors." He smiles and holds his beer to cheers me. I don't raise my can to him. He clinks mine anyway. I nudge Skye in the arm, interrupting her conversation with a guy sitting on the other side of her. "This jerk beside me is a total racist! He called my beer *NDN*!"

Skye leans over to look at him, laughs and says, "He is NDN!" Then holds her beer toward him, "Cheers, cuz."

"Who's your friend?" he asks Skye. Like I can't speak for myself. She's already turned back around. He stares at me and says, "I saw you and Skye at the mall last Friday." Then adds, "You were wearing a pink sweater." He's looking me in the eyes, attentive-like. Like I'm the only person in the room. Now that I'm no longer offended, I notice how good-looking he is. He has curly brown hair and blue-green eyes.

"Morgan Richards," is all I can think to say.

He holds out his hand. "Kevin Davies."

It feels like someone opened the window in a room I hadn't realized was stuffy. We chat about nothing particularly interesting, but I like how he speaks. He drags out his words, almost singsong-like. It's sexy.

FIRST CRUSH

Kevin lives one street over. His family moved here recently, which is why we'd never met before. He's a few years older than me and wears Polo cologne. *It smells so good.* I didn't know someone could *smell* handsome. It drives me wild.

The weekend after we met, we went for an afternoon walk through a trail, which ended with us making out. And last night when Skye and I went swimming, Kevin turned up at the pool with his buddy. He waved me over to the glass doors, then opened one a crack, careful the lifeguards wouldn't see. "We can meet you guys after swimming?"

"Sure," I answered, and returned to the pool. Then he had another question he forgot to ask. I walked over to them again, chatted, then climbed back into the water.

"They just want to see you in your bathing suit," Skye said, and swam away from me.

The way she said it, the way she swam away, I couldn't tell if she was being a friend or jealous.

It didn't take long before Kevin tried to do *it* with me. *But I was having none of it!* We had gone for a swim together, but instead of driving me home, he drove down to Seal Cove. We made out for a bit, and then things got heavy. I squirmed away and said I wanted to go home. It was uncomfortable being so isolated like that.

We never officially say we're "going out" or "a couple," but we start to spend a lot of time together. I'm thinking of introducing him to my dad, but he's been fishing a lot. I even start writing *Morgan loves Kevin* on my notebooks. It's so juvenile, but I can't help myself. He's my first real crush.

GUYS TALK

Skye isn't at school this morning, so I can't tell her about Seal Cove with Kevin. I'm studying alone in the back room when Nate comes walking in. It's been a while since we talked. I am sitting at a table, my textbooks spread around me. Nate's eyes go straight to my handwritten *Morgan loves Kevin*.

"That guy's a loser," he says, like those few words are a total waste of breath.

I say nothing.

"Have you done the Billy Joel assignment yet?" he asks, all casual, like he hasn't just dissed my love interest.

"No. I've been meaning to."

"I finished it. It was all right." He starts sharing historical details of the assignment — I have no idea what any of it means. Now he's telling me about the Suez Crisis.

The what?

He's talking about a canal in painstaking detail. The Mediterranean Sea, the Indian Ocean, and the Red Sea.

He may as well be speaking Chinese. Yet, I hang on to his every word. And think . . . my conversations with Kevin aren't nearly as stimulating. We talk about everyday stuff or gossip.

"Why are you going out with that guy?" he eventually asks, in a way that sounds like he's finally gotten to the point of why he's here.

"I'm not." I say it so quickly I surprise myself.

He side-eyes my notebook, again.

Why did you fool around with Skye? is what I want to ask him. "We're friends. We hang out." I can feel myself blushing.

"I heard." He gets up to leave.

Thankfully.

Then adds, "Guys talk."

TERRACE

The following Saturday, Dad and I decide to drive to Terrace. He needs a new winch for the boat. We take day trips there now and again since they have a better selection for shopping. Terrace isn't that nice, though. It's a total redneck town known for blatant racism. I haven't personally experienced it, but it's there. You can sense it. You see the way store clerks look down on Native people. It's sickening. Meanwhile, *who the hell are they?* Standing behind a counter laboring for barely five dollars an hour.

Dad drops me off at the mall before he goes to get his part. I take my time looking around in Kmart, grab a few things, and browse other stores I like. It's a mini-getaway. Then Dad picks me back up, and we head to Mr. Mike's Steakhouse — our usual routine.

We both order steak. Dad orders his medium-rare; me, well-done. It's past lunch, so we hit the salad bar like ravenous wolves. I fill my plate with carrot sticks and ranch dip. My dad eats weird vegetables like pickled beets and alfalfa sprouts. As if that isn't bad enough, he drizzles blue cheese dressing on top. We settle into our seats and dig in. Dad starts telling me about the parts he bought for the boat, and explains how he's going to install them. He puts down his fork and raises his hands as if he's holding the part. It's like he's mapping out a plan as he's telling me.

Our steaks arrive, and Dad sprinkles Lawry's Seasoned Salt on his baked potato. And after his first bite of meat, says, "You can't beat charbroiled." He says that every time.

After we're done eating, we head back to Rupert, arriving home in the early evening. Dad goes straight to his room to make a phone call and then says he's heading to the bar. I think he has a girlfriend. I chuckle at the thought. Most parents I know are married. I unpack my shopping bags and have a hot bath. Afterwards, I decide to watch *Casablanca*, which I'd rented from the library. Even though it's an old movie, a black-and-white, it's so good! "*Play it, Sam.*" I end up falling asleep on the couch.

PHONE CALL

The following afternoon, I'm cleaning the kitchen when my bedroom telephone rings. (Dad insisted I get my own number a few years back. He was tired of me holding up the line.) I run upstairs to grab it.

"Hey, Morgan, how's it going?" It's Aimee Johnson. She's a twin. She attends Alternate as well. Aimee's a lot of fun and loves to laugh. We've hung out a few times. She constantly says *"Oh my god!"* And she always seems to have some type of drama going on. Her mom won fifty thousand dollars at a big bingo last year. They got a brand-new car and furnished their townhouse rental. Everyone was happy for them, a single mom with four kids.

"How come you weren't out last night?" she asks.

"My dad and I went to Terrace."

We continue making small talk, then she says, "Hey, do you have Kevin Davies's phone number?"

"Hang on, I'll grab it." My coolness surprises me. I know his number by heart, but I wasn't gonna let her know that. Aimee and I aren't close friends or anything, but we play pool or foosball at school once in a while. She should know about Kevin and me. Why else would she be asking *me* for his number? What's worse, she didn't seem to see anything wrong with it. I give her the number, and we hang up.

GAINING CONTROL

For whatever reason, Bryan's taken a liking to me. It's late spring and he's been on my case about every assignment. Encouraging me to stay on top of things so I can attend PRSS for eleventh grade. He says it's important to reenter public school, and he thinks I'm ready.

Bryan enters the room this morning saying, "*Morgan Ashley, Morgan Ashley!*" He's waving a paper in his hand, like he is heralding headline news. He's hilarious. He overheard Skye calling me by my first and middle names once and made a big deal about it. *That's your full name?*

He shows me what subjects and scores I need to pass my exams. Then he tells me I have *unrealized potential*. As he leaves the room, he holds the paper up again and says, "You have what it takes, Morgan. You've got a bright future ahead of you!"

It's the first time I've been a "teacher's pet."

I have to admit, I don't hate it.

I feel like I'm finally gaining control of my life. It's a good feeling. School, Skye, and now Kevin. Well, except for that phone call from Aimee the other day! I've tried brushing it aside, but it's been nagging at me.

When Kevin and I meet up after school, I play it cool. That lasts about four minutes before I blurt out, "I hear you have a new *friend*."

"What are you talking about?" he replies casually.

"Aimee called me asking for your number."

"I met her at a party over the weekend." Then, in a blaming tone, he adds, "*You* gave her my number? You're the reason she's calling!"

"Whoops, sorry," I chuckle.

WHAT ABOUT THAT JONES BOY?

Dad's been working on the boat, doing maintenance. I try to help out now and again. Give the boat a good scrub down, or whatever else he needs help with. I'm not exactly the son he never had, but I try.

It's a sunny Saturday afternoon, so I decide to surprise my dad with lunch. I make my way down the wharf; there's nowhere quite like Prince Rupert's harbor when the sun's out. The water shimmers like a giant blue sapphire. Okay — I'm exaggerating slightly, but it is pretty.

I climb onto Dad's boat. I can hear Trooper's "General Hand Grenade" playing.

"Lunchtime," I announce, walking into the galley. I place the brown bag on the table. "Special delivery — burgers from La Gondola."

Dad comes down from the wheelhouse and does his signature dance move — the arm wave, with a cheeky grin on his face. I can't help but smile back. He's in a good mood for someone covered in engine grease. I've noticed he seems happier these days, and he's been going to the bar less.

"How did you know I was craving a burger?" he asks, reaching for the hamburger and tearing the wrapper off.

"Easy." I reply. "You're always in the mood for a burger." I'd forgotten to get us drinks. I go to the fridge to see what's in there.

"Grab me a beer while you're there, Morg."

My dad is pretty disciplined when it comes to drinking on the boat. He learned it from his father. It's allowed only on shore, one or two beers, usually after you're done work.

He cracks the can open and takes a swig. Then he starts looking out the window and gives someone a nod. I lean toward him to look out. Nate is walking by with his father.

"When are you going to get a boyfriend?" Dad asks "What about that Jones boy?"

"Dad! Please." I feel my cheeks flush. I have yet to tell him about Kevin. It's going on two months now.

"Okay, I'll stop!" He smirks, looking away.

Dad's T-shirt is covered with rust and oil. His carved-gold Native pendant hangs from a thick chain. It's an Eagle (Laxsgiik), his and Nana's crest. In Tsimshian culture, crests are matrilineal. Mine is a Wolf (Laxgibuu), the same as my mother's. He takes his last bite of burger, then wipes his hands on his jeans. "I have to go uptown and do some banking," he says. "Do you need money for shopping? Clothes, anything?"

"If you're offering." I smile, then shove a couple of fries into my mouth. I glance at his shirt. "And while we're at it, we should go to Mark's and get you some new tops."

SPILL IT!

The following Monday, I make my way to school. We only have a few weeks to go before the end of the year. Bryan told me I shouldn't have any problem passing my exams — then I'm off to PRSS in the fall.

Skye and I are sitting in the back room. She's strangely quiet this morning. And I keep catching her staring at me. "What?" I ask.

"Nothing." She glances down at her textbook.

I catch her looking again. "Spill it!" I snap. "What is it?"

"I take no delight in telling you . . ." The self-satisfied look in her eyes says otherwise. "Kevin and Aimee looked pretty cozy at a party over the weekend."

I feel nothing. No jealousy, no stomach pangs. "I'm not surprised," I say matter-of-factly. "She called me the other week asking for his phone number."

My indifference stumps Skye. Her eyes do a quick back-and-forth. Like she's trying to figure out what to come back with.

It's my turn to sit smug.

PANCAKES

Dad's leaving for fishing today, so I wake to the smell of him making us breakfast. Pancakes with all the fixings: bacon, maple syrup, whip cream, and orange juice. It's his specialty. After we dig in, he tells me about the latest book he's read — "*Dance Me Outside* by W.P. Kinsella" — and adds, "You should read it."

"Hmm," is all I reply. We don't usually like the same books.

"The author isn't Native," he continues. "But he sure as hell writes like he is."

I reach for the syrup and pour another generous amount on my pancakes. "Jess is graduating on Friday," I say, changing the subject.

"Oh, nice."

"Grad weekend should be fun," I add.

Dad always carries cash — hundreds of dollars at any given time. He reaches for his wallet and gives me spending money. "Be safe," he says.

I get up to clear the dishes. "Thanks, Dad. I will."

I drive my dad to the boat and help him bring his gear down. Before I leave, we hug and he says, "The opening's only forty-eight hours, but make sure and go to your grandparents'."

"Yeah," I mumbled. "And load 'er up, eh!"

He always tells me to go to my grandparents'. I never do anymore. Except for eating dinner now and again. I prefer to be on my own. Besides, Nana constantly drops in while Dad's away, checking up on me.

GRAD WEEKEND

Jess chose a cute strapless peach dress for graduation. And she got her hair done in a loose pin-up. She always has the latest style of clothing, and she wears carved-gold Native bracelets on each wrist. They're stunning pieces and go nicely with her gown. Jess's mom is Native, and her dad is white. She looks more like her mom than her dad. She's headed off to college in the fall. I'm super sad she's moving, but she's excited to attend Malaspina.

Grad weekend is a big deal in our little town. After the walk-up ceremony, everyone's in full-on celebration mode. There's going to be a bonfire party later tonight at the industrial site.

We load up on booze and head out with Jess's friends. When we arrive at industrial, the bonfire is already blazing. Fresh pallets had been thrown on the fire, and cars and trucks are parked in a circle around it. Massive speakers sit on top of one vehicle, blaring music. And car trunks are open for easy access to booze. I knew it would be a bash, but not this big a crowd. It's a mixture of mostly whites and some Natives.

Some of the grads stayed in their gowns and tuxedos. I am wearing a new calico floral dress from Mantique. It has buttons down the front and sits just above the knee, and I also splurged on new cognac leather slingbacks. My signature gold hoop earrings pull the outfit together.

"Morgan!" Skye waves me over. I wave back and make my way toward her. She looks gorgeous in a short black dress and cropped acid-washed jean jacket. She's with some new guy she's been hanging out with lately. He's way older and not the least bit handsome, but he has a car and money. "You're so hard to get a hold of these days!" she says, annoyed-like.

"I've been helping my dad on the boat." It's somewhat true. Truthfully, though, I haven't felt like hanging out with Skye. She was so eager to tell me about Kevin and Aimee. Like she enjoyed breaking the news to me. Or maybe it reminded me of what she and Nate did. Either way, it rubbed me the wrong way.

"Who are you here with?" she asks.

"I came with Jess and a bunch of her friends." We make more small talk, then I say, "I should get back, Jess is probably looking for me." A total lie. Jess is so social, she won't even have noticed I was gone.

"I'll come with you and say hi," Skye says, and loops her arm through mine.

I spot Kevin on the way back. He's standing with a group of guys smoking a joint. They're snickering through inhaled-exhaled breath. It's no wonder we never had any deep conversations. He was always fried out his head. What a turn-off. I heard he told people he *nailed* me. And he had a couple of girls on the go.

Good riddance!

The grad party is a fun night. I thought the cops would show up, but they didn't. I don't stay too late, though, and am glad there's a new program for grad weekend that provides volunteer designated drivers. I have no problem finding a ride home.

DISTRESS CALL

It's late Monday afternoon. I'm standing at the top of the wharf, and I still can't see my dad's boat. It's unusual for him to be returning so late. This morning, he said they were loaded and heading in, but that was ten hours ago. They should be here by now.

I already checked the cannery to see if they were unloading, but they weren't. I scan the harbor again. None of the boats coming in are his. I decide to call Nana from the phone booth to see if she's heard anything. I'd been hanging out with Skye all afternoon, so she might have been trying to reach me.

"Honey, where are you?" Nana's voice sounds frightened. Then she says, "We've been trying to get a hold of you."

"I'm down at the dock. Dad's not in yet."

I stare out at the gray sky.

"Come to our place, dear. Right away, okay, Morg?"

"*Why?*" I sound harsher than I mean to, but something in her voice makes me uneasy.

"Oh, sweetheart." Nan starts sobbing. "Just get here, now!"

"Nana," I yell. "Tell me what's going on right now!"

I can hardly make out her response. "A distress call went out . . . a boat rolled over at the narrows . . . Coast Guards responded . . . it was too late . . . no survivors were found."

It feels like the phone booth is spinning and closing in on me and like my legs are going to give out. I drop the phone. The last thing I hear is Nana wailing. I turn to leave, using the booth to steady myself, and I bump into Nate. His face is white as a ghost. "Morg-an." He chokes on his words. *He knows.* Of course he does. Other boats would have heard the distress call. I shake my head. "No." And push past him.

No. If I say *no*, then it can't be true. *No, no, no.* I run to my truck. Dad's old truck. He'd given it to me for my sixteenth birthday. It was practically brand-new. I turn the ignition and peel out of the parking lot. I glance at my rearview mirror. Nate's a blur, standing in the middle of the road. I turn the corner and start to feel dizzy. Like everything's spinning. I pull over and turn the truck off. I can't seem to think straight.

I stare at dust on the dashboard; the sudden silence is deafening. I don't know what to do with it.

I can hear Nana's wailing, her words echoing in my head, *rolled over at the narrows . . . no survivors*. I think of the two crew members on board. What are their names? How could I not remember? I want the sound of her crying to stop but I also want the silence to go away. I start hitting the steering wheel and scream. My screaming turns to strange-sounding sobs. *No!*

I hear a vehicle pull up behind me. I force myself to stop crying, which is surprisingly easy, because — *this isn't real*. How can it be? Their names are John and Gary. My dad's two deckhands. There's a gentle knock on my window. It's Nate. He motions me to move over. I slide to the passenger seat and he climbs in, starts my truck, and puts it into drive. Slowly, he makes his way toward my grandparents' place.

LOSS

I've grown up around loss. The first time I heard the word "suicide," I was five or six years old. We'd received a phone call in the middle of the night; a young boy had committed suicide on our reserve. He was my cousin's best friend. My dad hung up the phone and shared the news with my mom, not realizing I was listening from down the hall. I had an immediate visual of the way he died. And I remember the concern I felt for my cousin's loss. And the way he was never the same after that.

Our people have always suffered from loss.

It's all around us.

Loss of life from drinking and driving, senseless drunken brawls, broken hearts, grief, and cancer.

The list goes on and on.

Dad was always attending a memorial for some fishing or reservation buddy. So was Nana. Loss is a constant.

But you never think it will happen to you.

Now, here we are, facing an unbearable loss. A loss that doesn't seem real.

CELEBRATION OF LIFE

I am trying to remember. To remember the events from this past week. But it's all a blur.

I couldn't eat even though I was surrounded by food. People kept dropping off full meals at my grandparents'. Trays of sandwiches, homemade cakes, and cookies. It was helpful to have so much food on hand for all the visitors who stopped by.

I've been staying at my grandparents' house all week. This morning, I was up before them. I crept around, being sure not to wake them. God knows, they need the rest. I poured myself a cup of coffee — I don't even drink coffee — then reached for an apple turnover, and bit into it. Standing in the kitchen, I felt a moment of joy. The turnover was sweet and flaky in my mouth. I immediately burst into tears. *How can I enjoy food when my father is dead?*

The funeral service was held this afternoon. I was completely numb at the cemetery. I couldn't even cry. I've been vacillating between feeling numb and burning with rage. *Why him?*

We're now at the Moose Hall for my father's celebration of life. Now there's a misnomer. The last thing I feel is celebratory.

The hall is packed with fishermen and their wives and fellow members of the Native Brotherhood (Dad was a loyal member for years). I'm sitting on Nana's left; Grandpa is on the other side of her. He hasn't been handling my father's death well. He's lost his only son. My heart feels like it's being crushed by an unbearable weight, but it makes me downright sick to imagine Grandpa's grief. *All our grief.* But my dad had fished with Grandpa since he was a young boy. Even before taking him on the boat, they started rod fishing off the dock. Nana has a framed picture of them. And then they commercial fished together right up until Dad bought his own boat at thirty. Even then, Dad was always on Grandpa's boat helping him out. They helped each other out.

Nana's been putting on a brave face. Even in her grief, she has to look *just so*. Her head is held high, graciously nodding at mourners paying their respects. I know she's hurting, too. I think she's still in shock, like a deer in headlights. She's been fussing about Grandpa and me, making sure we are okay. I think it's her way of distracting herself.

Dad didn't believe in sitting around crying over the dead. When drinking, he'd say, "I want a celebration of life when I go, a big bash. Why not go out in style? Buy a round of Pilsner for the house."

Nana's friends have put out quite the spread. Dad appreciated good food; he would have approved. The speeches are over, thankfully. It was hard to listen to people talk about my father in the past tense, when I haven't entirely accepted he's gone. As the evening goes on, the mood becomes more relaxed. The air is filled with cigarette smoke, grief, and fishing stories. People start to mingle about, while Trooper's "Santa Maria" plays overhead. The volume is low, so no one has to raise their voices over the music. I make my way to the dessert table. I overhear a white guy standing nearby say to another white guy, "Did you know this song was written about Prince Rupert?"

"No, it's 'Here for a Good Time,'" the second guy replies matter-of-factly.

"People make that mistake. But it's *this one*. 'Santa Maria,'" the first guy says. Then adds, "I knew the guy whose boat they were on that inspired the song."

It's a musical tidbit I would have eagerly filed away to tell my dad. We loved to share music trivia with each other.

I think about the lyrics. "Sailed out on the Northern Sea." I guess that's what my dad did. I somehow feel a sense of peace. Just then, Nate walks past me, heading to the restroom. "Morgan." He nods, almost bows, and keeps on. He barely looked at me.

I notice people have been avoiding me. It's like they don't know what to say, so they stay away. Death makes people funny that way.

After I finished dessert, I say goodnight to my grandparents. I've had enough. It's time to go home. *Home, home.*

When I arrive, I walk straight to my bedroom, kick my shoes off, and break down and weep — an uncontrollable release of everything I've held in all day, all week.

I fall asleep, exhausted.

The following morning, Jess calls. Her parents said Dad's celebration moved to the Ocean View pub. They said it was a full house.

A true fisherman's send-off.

SUMMER

I don't like being at home. Everything reminds me of my father. It's his house. It isn't any better at my grandparents'. They're in pain, too, and I can't help but worry my presence makes them feel worse because they feel bad for me. It's like we are tiptoeing around one another's grief.

I avoid driving the waterfront route, as seeing boats in the harbor is a painful reminder. I know it doesn't make any sense; Rupert is surrounded by water. Jess invites me to Smiles Café for fish-and-chips, but I tell her I can't go near the water, not yet. She says she understands and suggests meeting for Chinese instead.

"What are you up to this summer?" she asks softly. Like she's afraid to ask the wrong question; she's another one who's been avoiding me since my dad died. I know I shouldn't think like that. And I'm grateful for the invite today. Anything to get me out of the house.

"I dunno." I shrug.

"Our plant's hiring — it's good money!" She smiles Then adds, "Come clean fish with me!"

"Yeah. Skye mentioned her plant is hiring, too." I push my food away. My appetite still hasn't returned. Everyone's been busy working at the cannery this summer, putting in long hours and making big bucks. Skye's first check was twelve hundred dollars! Jess says she's saving her money. She'll need it for college in September.

Meanwhile, I have nothing but time on my hands. Too many questions and not enough answers: Where am I going to live? Are we going to sell the house? And will this heaviness in my chest ever go away?

A KNOCK AT THE DOOR

It's the middle of August. And going on two months without my father. An entire salmon season without him. We didn't jar any fish. How could we? Preserving fish is a family tradition. Dad and Grandpa would catch the sockeye, gut and clean them, and then Nana and I would jar them. With help from the guys, of course! Nana and I are both too scared to operate the pressure cooker. We would jar cases and cases of fish every summer.

Nan said not to worry, though: We have enough from previous years. "Your dad made sure of that," she'd said with a smile. But the sadness in her eyes almost canceled her smile.

I have good days, where I feel okay. Others, I feel like a walking zombie.

Nana has been trying to get me to move in with them. "Morgan, honey, you're sixteen — you can't stay alone," she'd said recently.

I assured her that, for the time being, I was fine.

It's nearing lunch when I hear a knock at the door. I know it isn't Nana; she has a key. I go to open it — it's Nate.

"Hey," I say, pushing the screen door open.

"I have fish for you. We caught them this morning."

"Oh wow. Thank you, come in."

He enters and places a couple of sockeyes in the sink. "They're gutted, but I can cut them into smaller pieces or fillets for you."

"Um. Sure, fillets would be great." I go to the drawer and grab Dad's filleting knife, pull it from the sleeve and hand it to him, along with a cutting board, then move to stand at the opposite end of the counter. A reasonable distance from him. He starts cutting the fish, and I realize I'll need freezer bags. I grab them and start bagging. We stand side by side, silent. I'd forgotten these awkward feelings between us.

"I went out with my cousin. We didn't go too far, but we managed to catch a few."

"Thanks for thinking of me," I say.

"Are you hungry? Should we cook some up?" he asks.

"Sure, if you cook it." I smile.

"Of course. How should we make it?"

"Hmm, should we fire up the BBQ?"

He looks out at the rain.

"Our deck is covered," I quickly add.

"Sure, I can do that," Nate replies.

"And there's leftover potato salad."

"Perfect."

I finish bagging the fish and leave some pieces out for lunch.

Nate washes his hands at the sink and asks where our spices are. I point to the cupboard near where he's standing. He opens the cupboard door and examines its contents. Really examines. Then takes a few jars out. I notice how comfortable he seems in a kitchen. He starts telling me about fishing with his dad this summer, and how he receives half a crew share — which means he gets paid well.

He says he wouldn't bother with school if he had it his way, he'd rather fish full-time, but his mom won't allow it.

Thankfully, he doesn't bring up my father. It's still too hard to talk about.

We eat our meal sitting on the bar stools at the island, which feels less formal. Our kitchen, dining room, and living room are open-concept. The vaulted ceiling has exposed wooden beams. I become aware of how cozy the mood is, especially sitting with Nate. I almost feel happy.

When we're done eating, there's a sudden silence. I abruptly get up to clear our plates. I place them in the sink, rinse them, and walk into the living room.

Nate calmly follows. He has a relaxed manner, steady and grounded. He picks up a VHS from the coffee table and reads it, "*Lawrence of Arabia*. You found this at the library?"

"Yeah, have you seen it?" I ask.

"No, but I've been meaning to. Let's watch it," Nate says.

"Sure, I'm not going anywhere in this weather." I can hear the rain still coming down.

We're sitting on opposite ends of the couch, yet I feel the need to toss a pillow between us. An additional barrier, even if it's only imaginary.

We knew the movie was long, but not *three hours and forty-two minutes long*. I couldn't even tell you what it was about when it was over. It was hard for me to concentrate.

Nate shares his critique of the movie (hadn't we had enough?). "You can see why they say it's one of the best films ever made," he says.

"I liked Omar Sharif," I reply, and make an over-exaggerated yawn.

"I should go." Nate gets up from the couch.

I walk with him to the door. "Hey, thanks again for the fish."

"No problem. I can always bring more."

HER

Nana invites me for lunch. Grandpa is fishing, so I pull into his parking spot. My grandparents use their back door as the main entrance, so I walk into the kitchen and see a woman sitting at the table. The framed picture from Dad's dresser flashes into my mind. *It's her.*

My mother.

She's sitting at the table, cradling a cup of coffee with both hands. She's not as young as the picture but still looks the same. A rage immediately rises in my chest. "What the hell is she doing here?!"

"Morgan, dear, we have a visitor."

Nana is acting like this is any old visitor.

"Seriously, Nan, is this a joke? Why is she here?" I don't look in my mother's direction. I won't dare dignify her with a glance.

Nana's at a loss for words. Flustered, "Now, Morgan..."

I can't restrain myself. "Dad is dead. I don't know why the hell else she would be here?"

"I'd better leave," my mother says as she stands.

I still don't acknowledge her. "Is it for the house?!" I continue, my voice rising. "Because she's not bloody getting it!"

"Morgan, you stop!" Nana says, almost in shock.

I have to get out of here. My mother is still standing at the table, frozen-like. I turn to leave and slam the door behind me. The pebbles in the driveway make a cracking sound under my Doc Martens, like I'm pulverizing them with each step. I climb into my truck and pause before turning the ignition. I reach for the door handle, ready to go back inside, but for Nan's sake, I stop myself. Who knows what I'm capable of doing? I want to lunge across the table at her or flip it over. The feeling of rage quickly changes to confusion. Why the hell is my mother here? And did Nana actually think this was a good idea? Did she think I'd just sit down and join them?!

I turn on my truck and tear out of the driveway. Determined to get far from here. From *her*.

Hot Shots

I still can't listen to Trooper. It was Dad's favorite band. But it's unavoidable: Their *Hot Shots* album is playing everywhere in this damn town. I know the words to every song by heart. That's what happens when you've been exposed to it since birth. I'm housecleaning with the radio on. Trooper's "Baby Woncha Please Come Home" starts playing. I immediately think of my dad. The twangy-like instrumental part guts me.

I can't do nothin'
I can't feel nothin'
I can't be nothin'
without you

I picture my dad chair dancing. Handsome, with his cheeky grin. Wearing one of his old, faded T-shirts, his strong brown fisherman arms raised.

I allow the tears to fall.

THE EMPRESS

It's the second to last weekend of summer, Skye and I are looking to blow off steam. I've been feeling the need ever since my mom showed up earlier in the week. Nana and I never did talk about that day. We acted like it never happened.

Skye's family hangs out at the Empress. It's a total dive bar. I'm talking *dive* — a glass of beer is a dollar. But her grandmother is considered royalty there — Empress Royalty.

Skye often pokes her head in the door when we're downtown, usually to say hello, but mainly to get spending money from her mom.

When she peeks inside this time, sure enough, her family is there. She walks in and goes straight to their table. I follow along, even though we're not nineteen. I've never been in here before, so I take a quick glance around the room. A stench immediately invades my nostrils. It's a mixture of stale beer, cigarettes, and old carpet. Skye sits down on a black vinyl chair with wooden armrests. She eyes the jug of draft beer on the table and says to her mom, "Buy us some *real* beer."

Her mom's feeling good, a bit tipsy. She hesitates but quickly gives in — Skye is her favorite. She walks over to the bar, and soon after, returns with two bottles of Budweiser. "Is this what you kids drink these days?" She smiles, setting them down in front of us.

No.

"Thank you." I smile back.

"Gran, cheers us," Skye says. She holds her bottle toward her grandmother. We cheers their cheap glasses of beer; they, our expensive bottles. A popular old song starts playing. Skye's grandma immediately starts hooting and hollering, and says, "Come on, girls!" She has a deep smoker's voice.

The bar is nearly empty. I can hardly believe I am here, let alone drinking a beer. *And now I'm supposed to dance?* Sometimes, friendship with Skye is challenging.

I have no time to give it further thought. Skye is already standing and pulling at my sleeve. "You heard her!"

Her grandma's heavier, wearing a silky pink blouse. Her short silver hair is teased high, and she's givin'er on the dance floor. So is Skye. Her grandma cheers even louder once I join them. I have no choice but to get into it, too.

A few patrons start to cheer us on. To my surprise, I realize — *I'm having fun.*

Suddenly, Skye has an embarrassed look on her face. She rushes to my side and says, "Look over in the back corner!"

I follow her eyes. Nate and some boys from school are sitting around a small table, facing the dance floor. A white boy named Jared is cheering the loudest. He's whistling with two fingers in his mouth, and fist pumping with his other hand. Skye waves them over to join us.

Before you know it, Nate is dancing in front of me, with a big smile on his face. White-boy Jared is dancing with Skye's grandma; the other Native boy, Geoff, is with Skye and her mom. We're all boogying up a storm. Then Skye eyes me and nods toward the bar. The bartender and server are talking and looking in our direction. One of them heads over, likely aware we're not old enough. Which is obvious. Five underage kids on the dance floor of an otherwise empty bar.

Skye quickly kisses her mom and grandma goodbye, and we race for the door, the boys following behind us. The lyrics to "Wooly Bully" ring out, as if chasing us. We burst out into the street, laughing. It's still daylight out. We squint our eyes, adjusting after being in a darkened barroom. "You guys blew our cover! They were serving us all afternoon!" Jared slurs.

"Hey, man, the party didn't start until we showed up." Skye laughs.

PRSS

Back to school. I thought I had been coping with my father's death for the most part. The painful sting "lessening." But at times, overwhelming grief washes over me. And it happens so suddenly, unexpectedly. Like Labor Day weekend — Dad and I would have been in Vancouver doing some back-to-school shopping, eating at fun restaurants, and going to the PNE. In their grief, and being newer guardians, my grandparents didn't think to offer me money for school clothes. Thankfully, I had enough to buy a few outfits at Mantique, but I wasn't interested in shopping, anyway. I didn't even want to go to school. PRSS or Alternate. I just didn't.

Returning to senior high feels like a foggy haze. I'm going through the motions. That's it. I don't like constantly shuffling between classrooms. Different teachers and classmates in every room. Two weeks in, I find myself back at Alternate. Sitting in Bryan's office, a miserable look on my face.

"We were sorry to hear about your father, Morgan. We really were." He can't look at me when he says it. "Of course, we're always here to help, but there is a counselor at PRSS. I can introduce you."

"I don't need *help*. I just don't want to go to school there," I mutter.

"You should give PRSS a go." He's looking me in the eye now. "Reintegrating into senior high is best for your future. It's best for the long term." Then adds, "Make an appointment with the counselor there."

I give it another *go*. I even go and say hello to the counselor. He just stares out at me from behind his desk. Maybe because I stand the entire time. Looking around his office at his books and art. Questioning him about them.

But it's no use. I hate senior high. I don't understand math or science. I have nothing in common with a bunch of phony white kids. All their designer-brand clothes and big hair. Their problem-free lifestyles. Did their father die over the summer holidays? Did their mother return after abandoning them for years? Years. Nothing makes sense. After one month, I drop out of eleventh grade. I don't bother telling Bryan that I couldn't *reintegrate*.

SKYE

Skye is house-sitting at her older brother's place. She's invited me over to hang out. When I knock on the front door, I hear music playing. I know she won't hear me, so I let myself in. The sound is coming from the kitchen. Skye's singing at the top of her voice to "Ti Amo" by Laura Branigan. She isn't much of a music person, but she loves this song. It's all right at best. "Hello, I'm here," I call out.

The singing stops.

I enter the kitchen. Skye's sitting at the table looking out the window. A can of Pilsner is in front of her. I slide into a chair across from her. There's an energy in the room I can't place. I glance out the window, unsure where else to look. As the song comes to an end, Skye says, "Beer's in the fridge."

It's three o'clock on a Tuesday afternoon, but I go to the fridge, grab a beer, and return to the table. I crack it open and take a swig. "*Ahhh!*" I exaggerate.

"Cheers, bitch." Skye holds her can toward me.

Skye is the strongest person I know. She doesn't live with either parent. She never has in all the time I've known her. She bounces from her brothers to her sisters, different friends' places, or boyfriends, when she has one. She is Teflon tough. Not just physically (especially for being so skinny), but mentally, too. She doesn't let anything get to her. Which is why the energy in the room is so uncomfortable. And she has a blank, lost look in her eyes.

"How come you're not in school?" I manage.

"I got kicked out yesterday," she says and looks back out the window.

"Is that what we're celebrating? I'll drink to that." I take another sip.

Skye chuckles, "Nah, I can't be bothered with that place anymore. I've been kicked out of school more times than I can count." Then says, "I went to my aunt's over the weekend. Your mom was there."

"Oh yeah," I reply coolly. I'd heard she was still in town.

"We had an interesting conversation. We talked for hours."

"What the hell, Skye. Why would you even talk to her?"

Skye is rarely serious and hardly ever talks about the deeper things in life. For the most part, she enjoys laughing and having a good time, but she isn't kidding around now. She looks me in the eye, takes a slow, deliberate sip, and looks back outside. "You know they used to take Native people away from their families and send them to those residential schools, right?"

I nod. "Yeah." And shift in my chair.

"Did you know your mom was sent to one?"

"My dad mentioned it."

"Did you know they sexually abused kids there?"

"I heard they didn't treat them well," I reply, wondering where she's going with this, and hoping she gets there quick.

"Did you know your mom was sexually abused there?" Her eyes are fixed on mine.

I can't hold her gaze. I look outside and focus on the rain.

"Even a nun tried to assault her. She had to fight her off."

"Skye, what the fuck? *I don't want to hear this!*"

"That's why she left here, Morgan."

"Lots of people went to those schools, Skye. They didn't leave their families to become skid-row drunks," I yell.

"Your mom said Main and Hastings is full of them. Lost souls, too broken or ashamed to go home. Or they were taken so young that *they don't remember where home is*."

I don't want to continue this conversation, but I don't know how to end it. Skye isn't someone to mess around with.

Skye takes a drag of her smoke and exhales. "And your mom *isn't* a skid-row drunk."

"Oh, you're suddenly the expert?!" is all I can think of.

"The reason she left town, left you and your dad, is . . ." — she clears her throat — "she was raped at a party."

"Skye! I don't want to talk about this!"

"You need to hear this, Morgan. That rape triggered her." Skye's eyes are no longer lost but full of painful emotion. "Your mom blocked out the abuse from residential school until . . . until . . . that happened to her." She stares down at the table.

The shabby kitchen suddenly feels suffocating, like it's closing in on me.

"I don't know how she blocked it out," Skye continues. "You don't forget something like that." Her last sentence is almost a whisper.

The room becomes filled with the most empty, hollow feeling.

Then Skye clears her throat again and continues, "Your mom sharing really helped me. I couldn't block it out, but I wouldn't dare talk about it." She stares at her beer can as she speaks.

I look at her.

"Skye, I'm sorry. I didn't know . . ." is all I can manage.

Neither of us say another word. I can't process all she's said, never mind come up with something comforting to say. We continue to drink our beers, listen to music, and stare out at the rain or the table. Anywhere but each other.

Skye eventually breaks the silence. "Time for another?" She gets up and walks to the fridge.

I get our next round, and the one after that.

When "We're Here for a Good Time" starts playing, Skye raises her head and starts howling like a wolf. I throw my head back in laughter, get up, and pull Skye up by the hand to dance.

Our socks easily glide on the worn linoleum floor, making me feel like a better dancer. We let loose, give in to the music and dance and dance and dance. The song may not be about Prince Rupert, but — it's still ours.

We get drunk. Gloriously drunk. *Luk'wil siin*, my dad would have said. We dance some more, laugh, and cry. Sitting on the floor, leaning against the cupboards, we both let out drunken sobs, look at each other's snotty-faced tears, and start to laugh.

NANA

Nana makes txadzemsk and homemade annay for lunch. We sprinkle chopped seaweed onto our bowls of soup and add extra oolichan grease. She doesn't use a lot when cooking because Grandpa can't eat much. We tease him, saying it's 'cause he's white. He's not tough like us.

We finished eating and linger at the table. "Nana, didn't you go to those residential schools?" I ask.

Nana stands abruptly and starts to clear the table. "You already know that I did, dear."

"Did you know my mom went there?"

"Yes, of course."

She's at the sink running water and clanking dishes like she's trying to drown me out.

I can't bear seeing her so uncomfortable. I decide to drop the subject, and I walk to the sink. "I'll do those, Nan. Go finish watching your show."

SOLID PLAN

I'm standing, holding the front door open for Nate. He's brought over a fresh spring salmon. Just as he's walking in, Skye drives up in her sister's little beater. She doesn't even have her driver's license. I wave and tell her to come in. Nate turns and nods as well. She rolls down the window and a smile spreads across her face. She yells out, "I'll come back later," and drives off.

It's been a few weeks since I last saw Nate. The time at the Empress with Skye. I am glad to see his face when I open the door. I find myself thinking about him more and more these days.

"Whoa, that's a huge fish," I gush.

Nate places it in the sink. "Should I fillet it?"

"Sure." I smile.

As he cuts up the fish, he starts telling me how school is going. Then says, "We miss seeing you, though."

"Yeah, it's just not something I can do right now."

"I understand."

"Did you hear Skye was kicked out?" I ask.

"I did hear that."

I watch as he fillets the fish like a pro.

"Do you want a beer?" I ask, making my way to the fridge. They're my dad's. They've been sitting around long enough. *The guy brought me fish; it's the least I can do*, I rationalize to myself.

"Sure."

I hate that I'm starting to feel nervous. I slow my movements, then hand him a beer and crack one open for myself.

When we're done bagging the fish, Nate offers to cook us dinner. Of course I accept.

He bakes spring salmon with garlic and lemon, and we eat it with rice and sweet pickles as a side. The conversation flows easily over dinner. We talk about fishing, school, Jackie Collins, and even my dad. I also tell him my grandparents decided to rent the house out, and that I'll be moving in with them. He says that sounds like a solid plan, then smiles at me. And I don't look away.

GARAGE SALE

We have a huge garage sale. Huge. Grandpa takes what he wants from Dad's stuff beforehand and prices the rest of the tools and fishing gear. It's late October — we're glad the forecast called for no rain — but we still keep most things for the sale in our opened garage. Skye is a big help, running around trying to push items. Convincing people they need things that they probably don't. She loves my grandparents, and they like her. Nate also comes to help. I tell him he can take whatever fishing stuff he wants. He says he'll wait until the end. My grandparents seem happy to have Nate around, asking how his family is doing and about fishing.

The sale is a lot of work, but also fun. We make seventeen hundred dollars. At the end of the day, Nate has his buddies pick up the remaining stuff, to take to the thrift store and the dump. Grandpa is impressed. He expresses his gratitude to Nate and offers him money. Nate politely declines.

I return to the house the next day. It's almost empty. It's a beautiful home. I haven't stopped to look at it in a while. It's the only home I've known. Walking through the house doesn't sadden me. Maybe because Dad's stuff isn't everywhere as reminders. Or because we aren't selling it — just renting it out for now. Yet at the same time it hits me: All his things are gone now, like him.

I try not to think about my dad's accident. I overheard Grandpa talking about insurance the other day. I also heard him telling Nana he was leasing Dad's fishing license. I walked into the kitchen and acted like I hadn't heard their conversation. Grandpa quickly changed the subject.

I see an envelope by the front door; I must have walked over it when I came in. I go to pick it up and open it. It's a handwritten letter. I shuffle to the last page; it's from my mother.

THE LETTER

Dear Morgan,

I've rewritten this letter so many times. I don't expect you to understand or forgive me. But I have to write.

I'll never forgive myself for leaving. But with help, I have decided to stop punishing myself for it. I can't begin to explain the damaged place I was in when I left. You have to imagine how bad things were to make me give up the life we had. What happened to me had nothing to do with you or your father; it happened long before you guys came along.

I didn't feel worthy of a beautiful family like ours or worthy of your father's love. That probably doesn't make sense to you; I can barely comprehend it myself. But drinking numbed the pain. Made me feel less broken. Less damaged. Allowed me to forget. That isn't an excuse — I know leaving was wrong.

Both my parents attended Indian residential school. They became alcoholics as a result of the trauma they endured. I have no real memories of them. My brother and I were also sent to residential school. I was five, and my older brother Ricky was six. Sadly, he died at the school. I never returned home again, back to the rez. With Ricky gone, I didn't think anything was there for me. When I left the school at seventeen, I moved to Vancouver. Shortly after, I met your father.

I wrote to your dad last year. Completely broken. I shared everything that happened to me at residential school. I provided my phone number, and he called me a few months later. We talked for hours. That conversation helped me get on the path to healing.

I moved to East Vancouver and started working at a place called Helping Spirit Lodge. They help women. For the first time in a long while, things felt okay. When I heard about your dad, I was completely grief-stricken. Broken. That news was too painful to bear. I left my job and made my way here. Morgan, I am so sorry for your loss. Your father was a special man, and I loved him very much.

I'm sorry to unload this on you. You didn't ask for any of this. But I need you to know I never meant to hurt you, and I've never stopped loving you, thinking about you, and praying for you.

Love, Mom

ANGER

I've read my mom's letter so many times. I don't know what I expected to unearth, by rereading. Yet there I found myself, poring over every sentence, even turning and staring at the blank back page. Mining for all that was lost.

I've tried writing her back. It always ends with me crumpling the page and throwing it in the wastebasket. At first, it was angry, crazy talk — I wrote the most outrageous, cruelest things. I was really venting.

You're nothing but a drunken skid-row bitch.

I would have broken the tip if I'd used a sharpened pencil. That's how hard I wrote. But to my surprise, the more I wrote, the better I started to feel.

CHANGES

I've settled into my grandparents' basement. It's a large rec room, which used to be Grandpa's space to watch TV. My grandparents bought me new furniture for it. Nana and I had fun picking stuff out. "Get the matching lamps," Nan said, "and that brass standing mirror." I put my foot down when she started trying to pick art for my walls. I also have my own full bath. We kept the living room section layout the same and set my bedroom up toward the back. It doesn't feel like home yet, but it's comfortable and familiar.

I do my best to stay out of their way. I mainly go upstairs to eat, but even that I keep to a minimum. I've always been close to my grandparents, and they're loving and kind, but living here is another reminder that Dad is gone. I see their grief close-up, and they, mine.

They provide me with a generous weekly allowance, so Skye and I have been going out to eat. We'll share a hamburger and fries at West End, a chow mein bun at New Moon, or a pepperoni pizza at Zorba's.

We've gotten closer since she shared what happened to her, even though we've never talked about it again.

She also confessed to me that she was the one who came on to Nate. And that they'd both had a lot to drink.

REVOLUTIONARY

We're halfway through November, and the rain, cold, and wind have been brutal. Nate and I have been hanging out more and more. He even talked me into returning to Alternate School. Thankfully, Bryan accepted me back.

Nate is incredibly bright. Anytime I praise him for it, he says, "My mom's a teacher. She encouraged me to read."

I read, I thought to myself. Yet I feel none the wiser for it.

He offers to help me catch up on my schoolwork, and he does.

It's Friday night. Nate has come over and brought pizza and some CDs he recently bought. He's playing a song, "Fight the Power" by Public Enemy. "Listen closely to the lyrics," he says.

After a few minutes I say, "I don't like rap. It's a bunch of noise."

"It's not," he replies. "They're radicals, sharing a revolutionary message."

Revolutionary. I stare at him. "Calling Elvis simple and plain is radical, all right."

Nate laughs. "The music video is awesome, too." He reaches for his bag and pulls out a hardcover book. "I finished reading *The Autobiography of Malcolm X*. You can borrow it."

"Who's he?"

"Hunny," he says with a soft chuckle, "you should try reading something other than Jackie Collins."

He's never called me a pet name before. It rolled off his tongue so naturally, too. I pretend to give him an uppercut to the rib. He winces like I'm hurting him.

"Hey, man," I say, trying to save face, "I followed the Nelson Mandela headlines!"

Nate smiles and pulls me toward him on the couch. In one swoop, I'm lying under him, and he's kissing me. He's held my hand while walking before, but he's never tried to kiss me. I wasn't ready then, and he likely sensed it. He's kissing me, softly, slowly. His hand is behind my head, holding it at an angle. I can't tell if I'm going to melt or explode. He stops and stares at my face, like he's trying to take in every inch of it. He moves my hair away from my face. I lean up to him, eager, but our teeth meet first. We both laugh. He slides his hand down my back and shifts me so we're both lying on our sides. We stare at each other for a while, our eyes saying so much. Then he kisses my forehead and pulls me closer. It surprises me how easily my body relaxes into his.

FAMILY DYNAMICS

Rereading my mom's letter over the past few days has somehow made me feel better. Well, not *better* but, in a way, at peace. The part where she explains why she left my father and me. Especially knowing that my dad knew. He knew we weren't the reason she left. It wasn't because we weren't good enough.

If I think back far enough, I realize I've always felt like something was missing. Even when my mom was here. I'd chalked it up to being an only child, but I don't think that was it. Knowing what I know now, I think my mother was always gone. She was with us but wasn't. And the way both my parents partied. They were equally seeking to feel less "numb," to "forget."

Even though my father didn't attend those schools, his

mother did. I love Nana, but I'm sure being raised by her wasn't easy.

Skye said nuns made students scrub the school from top to bottom. It made me think of how spotless my mother kept our home. Immaculate. Not only my mom, but Nana does this, too. Of course, a clean home is important, but I'm talking sterile. And there's a compulsiveness to it. Nana also obsesses over appearances.

Everything has to look *just so*.

And she discourages me from spending time in the sun. She tells me to scrub my neck and behind my ears, pumice my knees and elbows. *Use lemon*. Or she constantly reminds me to sit up straight. I took it as an annoying, nagging-grandmother thing, but I bet that's how those nuns spoke to her.

And maybe that's why Nana's constantly pestering her younger brother, Uncle Stuart. He also attended residential school. He's a lifelong bachelor, and I never understood why. He's an extraordinarily handsome, gentle, and kind man. But he keeps his home in total disarray! I've never seen a house as disorganized as his. There's stuff everywhere. His home is filled with books, Japanese glass floating balls, and other nautical items, like brass portal mirrors and anchors. Grandpa called him a "beatnik" once. Uncle Stuart's voice is measured, his speech is methodical, he doesn't waste words. He responded, "That's white man talk."

Maybe his unconventional lifestyle is a way for him to forget. Forget those rigid, stark rules that were forced upon him. A way to buck the system.

SHE'S BEAUTIFUL

My grandparents are in Hawaii for the month of January. They invited me to join them, but I thought they could use the break. These past few months have been hard. Christmas especially. Grandpa insisted we put up a tree. Nana and I went through the motions, but it wasn't much of a Christmas. How could it be?

Besides, Hawaii wouldn't have been the same without my dad. He loved it there so much. Always pronounced it *Hawai'i* like the Native Hawaiians. He could even pronounce the state fish of Hawaii — *humuhumunukunukuapua'a*. He'd practiced and practiced it until he finally got it.

I need a clothes organizer for my closet, so Nate offers to help pick one out and assemble it for me. We are leaving Zellers when I spot her.

My mother.

Even though she's older, her face is still youthful. She has a natural glow, dewy skin, and rosy cheeks. There's also a comfortable ease to her demeanor. Nate's carrying the organizer under one arm, and his other hand is resting on my shoulder. When she sees us, her eyes light up. Nate notices. He looks at her, then at me, then back at her, and gives her the nod. I hold her stare for a moment. I feel my face softening, but I keep walking.

In the parking lot, Nate asks, "Do you know that woman?"

"She's . . . my mother."

He opens the passenger-side door for me. Waits as I get in, and then, before closing it, he asks, "You okay? You wanna talk about it?"

"No, I'm fine." I give him a smile.

He gets in and starts the truck and slowly makes his way out of the parking lot. "You look a lot like her," he says.

I nod.

Then he adds, "She's beautiful."

REVOLUTIONARY APPROACH

Nate's telling Bryan about the latest book he's reading. "It's about a Black boxer who was wrongfully imprisoned." He continues, "He wrote the book in prison — it's called *The Sixteenth Round*." Nate grows quiet, then says, "The things that happen in the U.S. . . . it's unbelievable."

"I'll have to give it a read," Bryan responds.

"You know the Bob Dylan song 'Hurricane'?" Nate asks.

"Of course, it's a great song."

"It's written about this guy, Rubin Carter!"

"Oh, right," Bryan says while jotting down the book title.

I've never met a guy like Nate before. Not only has he read the classics (his all-time favorite book is *Great*

Expectations), but he also cares about injustices. And refers to a rap group as "revolutionary." Who talks like that?

Bryan hasn't been involved in my schooling since I returned. I thought it was because he was disappointed in me for returning to Alternate, but I think it's because Nate and I are always studying together. He knows I'm getting the encouragement and support I need.

I approached Bryan about letting Skye come back. He said they'd given her every chance available, but if she didn't want to accept help, there was nothing more they could do.

I decide to try a *revolutionary* approach. "Skye is a radical," I tell him. "It means she sees the world differently."

A sympathetic smile spreads across Bryan's face.

I feel my cheeks flush. Nate and his damn rap songs.

MY DAD

My grandparents are back from Hawaii. Nana is so tanned she's almost bronzed! It makes me a wee bit jealous. She looks nice and rejuvenated. Meanwhile, poor Grandpa is red as a lobster. I made them fish and rice for dinner as a welcome back. They were so happy and said they had been craving it. And made *mmm* sounds for their first few bites.

I thought about my dad a lot while they were gone. And my mother. And what I now know of her painful upbringing. It felt like the first time I had been alone with my thoughts. Really alone, to process things.

After my mom left, my dad stayed single. The only thing he did was fish and drink. He made a lot of money and blew as much partying. Easy come, easy go. He eventually started "seeing" women. But nothing serious; he never introduced me to any of them. Around six months before he passed away, I noticed he wasn't partying as much. Then I heard he was dating someone. I didn't know her but recognized her from around town. She wasn't beautiful like my mom or anything. She was white and kinda plain-looking.

I heard she was a secretary at City Hall, divorced with two young kids. I saw her at my dad's funeral from afar — she looked like a heartbroken woman. I was too overcome with grief to introduce myself.

Over breakfast the next morning, I decide to ask Nana about her. "Did you know the woman Dad was seeing before he passed?"

"Jill, she was nice. Really smart, too," Nana responds.

"How did you meet her? Did Dad introduce you?"

Nana smiles. "It's a small town, Morg. People know each other."

"I know *that*. But did Dad introduce her to you?"

"When Grandpa and I were at the pub, they'd come say hello or join us for a drink."

I consider her words for a moment. "Do you think he was planning on introducing me?"

"I think so. They were starting to get serious." Nan cups her hands over mine. "You were his pride and joy,

Morgie. He wouldn't bring anyone into your life unless she was *the one*."

I feel a lump in my throat. My dad used to listen to Marvin Gaye's "Pride and Joy" and he'd sing to me. I'd forgotten until Nana mentioned it. I smile thinking about him.

"I'm happy he found someone. I'm just sorry he didn't feel he could share that with me."

"They were taking things slow. Jill has two small kids and works full-time."

I get up from the table and stand behind Nana, wrap my arms around her and give her a tight squeeze. It feels good that we can talk about my dad.

IT'S FOR YOU

It's the end of March, and we've been having unusually nice weather. Skye's suddenly interested in bike riding. This latest amusement has come out of nowhere.

Neither of us own a bike, so we have been borrowing them from her brother. They're ugly and spray-painted and likely stolen. But we've been having a lot of fun. We bike along the old train tracks at Rushbrook and sometimes around town.

And Nate and I have been spending a lot of time studying together. It feels good to be taking my studies seriously. I feel less aimless. More confident. And it's addictive — like, the more I learn, the more I want to know. Nate's intellectual curiosity is really rubbing off.

Saturday morning, he calls to say he's on his way. Grandpa is working on the boat, and Nana is out grocery shopping. I'm at the kitchen sink washing my dish when Nate pulls up. I wave to him from the window. He has a larger-than-usual smile on his face as he climbs out of his truck and waves at me to come outside.

He's pulling a mountain bike from the back of his truck as I make my way toward him. It's a Kuwahara brand, neon purple with white accents.

"Cool bike!" I exclaim.

"It's for you." He smiles.

"What?!"

"Now you won't have to borrow Skye's brother's bike."

"Nate, no, it's too much!"

"It's not. I got a good deal. Try it out."

I climb on the bike and look at him.

"The height looks about right," he says, eyes moving from the seat area to the ball of my foot touching the ground.

I let it roll down the driveway, my legs out to the sides.

"Your feet go on the pedals," he calls out.

I start pedaling. "It's so smooth," I yell back. I ride to the end of the block, turn around, and make my way back just as Nana is pulling into the driveway.

"Nate, hi, dear," she says as she climbs out of her car. "Came to see our Morgan, did you?"

"Look what Nate got me, Nana." I sit tall and proud.

"Nate, you're going to spoil her!" Nan says. Then adds, "But that's okay, because we love our Morgie." She quickly kisses me on the cheek and walks toward the house, then turns to ask, "Are you kids going to want lunch? I'm making clam chowder."

I look at Nate, and he nods. "Yes, please," I reply.

We study, eat lunch with Nana, and study some more. At the end of our session, Nate says he is proud of how hard I've worked. And tells me I'm smart.

Oh, and we make out for a bit, too. I enjoy those sessions the best.

NATE'S FAMILY

Nate is close with his family. He's always talking about them or willingly hanging out with them. Even when complaining about his sister, he does it in a playful sibling rivalry way. He says he wants me to meet his parents. I tell him I need more time.

We went for pizza the other night. I surprised myself when I opened up about my mom, sharing that she had attended an Indian residential school. He listened closely and seemed genuinely saddened. He said he didn't know much about the schools, but he'd heard stories.

No one in his family attended the schools. His great-grandfathers on both sides hid their families from the Indian agent. His mother's grandfather took them fishing — they were at sea when the Indian agent arrived. His father's grandfather hid the kids at their family's mink trapping spot. He said the Indian agents repeatedly returned to round up kids. Each time, they were at sea. He also said it took great courage to hide them. If his great-grandfathers had been caught, they would have faced a major fine or been sent to jail. Then he said, "And not everyone's circumstances allowed them to hide their children. My family was just lucky."

I sat quietly. It strikes me that these schools weren't that long ago. *Some are still operational!* Yet no one talks about them. It's 1991. If my mother hadn't written me that letter or spoken with Skye, the topic of Indian residential schools wouldn't have come up. I'd heard little about the schools over the years, mainly just overhearing my dad when he was drinking. That's the only time he talked about it. And the way Nana fidgeted when I tried asking her about it? It seems no one wants to discuss the topic.

I don't blame them. It sounds like those schools were horrible. Nate's family didn't attend them. Maybe that's why they seem "normal."

CANOEING

Skye is in another one of her adventurous moods. This time, she's invited me to canoe at Prudhomme Lake. She said she went with her brother last week and it was a lot of fun. Her uncle lent her the fiberglass canoe; he left it hidden at the lake. He's not her real uncle, more like one of her mom's exes.

So, here we find ourselves, paddling in the middle of a damn lake. Then, I almost tip us over with a sudden jerky movement. We both scream, grasping the sides of the boat. I eventually get the hang of it. And once I do, it amazes me how peaceful it is. The lake somehow hushes you. Like the deep woods. You naturally lower your voice. I've spent a lot of time on the ocean but rarely on lakes.

We are fortunate the sun is out and it's warm enough for T-shirts. In April! We end up staying out for over an hour. Skye could have stayed a bit longer, but my arms were turning to rubber.

We pull the boat ashore and sit to rest on the sand. "We made it." I laugh quietly to myself and then start stretching my arms.

"You'll get used to it," Skye says.

"Man. It's beautiful out here." I lean back, taking in the scenery.

"It is. I'm glad my brother told me about the boat."

We stare at the water. The lake is still, placid.

"Have you responded to your mom's letter yet?" Skye asks.

I'd let her read it a while back. "No."

"I can't get over how evil that place was." She stresses the "evil." "Your mom was a little girl, and those nuns told her she was ugly. *Ugly!*"

I say nothing.

"*Who the fuck says that to a kid?*" Her voice is low but exact. "And they called her a good-for-nothing Indian and told her her parents were drunks and didn't want her."

I feel her words in my throat. I didn't expect them to pain me like that.

"Look at how gorgeous your mom is, Morgan. She's beautiful, but she doesn't know it. What's worse, she's a *good* woman, but probably doesn't know that either. It's so fucked up."

We sit in silence, again, without words.

CASHMERE NDN

I climb into Nate's truck and see a catalogue on the seat. I've never heard of J.Crew before. It's not a girly magazine or anything, but there's a woman on the cover. As he starts to drive, I pick it up and leaf through it. It looks expensive and uptight. They probably don't even sell sweatshirts (my go-to wear). I toss it aside.

"My family orders wool and cashmere sweaters from there."

"I've never heard of a cashmere-wearing NDN before. What, are we in a *Seinfeld* episode?" I say coolly.

He laughs. "I love that show."

Nate is hard to read. He's hardly a dark horse, but he has so many layers to him. His ex-girlfriend is white. *Whiter than white.* He hangs out with popular white kids from high school; then he turns around and rolls with Native kids from Alternate. *He attends Alternate!*

Last week, he was wearing a T-shirt with Elijah Harper on it. "Is that the guy with the feather from the news?" I'd asked him.

"*The guy with the feather*," he'd replied. "You mean, Aboriginal leader, MLA, Elijah Harper, who almost single-handedly stopped the Meech Lake Accord?"

"Sheesh. Excuse me," I grumbled.

"I'm sorry, hunny," he replied. "He's just such an important figure in our community." Then added, "Shirt's pretty cool, hey? I bought it off a Native guy on Granville Street."

I'd felt like such an idiot. But I barely watch the news.

My intelligent, well-read, cashmere-wearing fisherman boyfriend. He's like a kaleidoscope, *an enigma*. Sheesh, I'm starting to sound like Bryan with my fancy words.

Nate interrupts my deep thoughts. "Did you want to order something from the catalogue?"

"I like Sears," I respond dryly.

NOT A BIG DEAL

Not only has Skye refused to come back to school, but she's also started going out with a drug dealer. She claims she's madly in love and has already moved in with him. Troy is a black-leather-jacket-and-Dayton-boots-wearing kind of guy. He's a few years older than she is — older as in he has a mustache.

When I tell her I'm worried about her, she replies, "It's marijuana, Morgan — it's not a big deal."

She invites me over to their place. A handful of people are sitting in the living room when I arrive. Headbanger-type guys. They're passing a joint around, their eyes already glazed over. A few posters of metal bands are on the otherwise sparse walls. An empty Texas Mickey of Jack Daniel's is displayed on a floor speaker like it's a prized trophy. Troy acknowledges my presence with a nod.

Skye's new friends make me uncomfortable. I can't imagine striking up a conversation with them. What could we possibly talk about? And what makes me more concerned is, what does Skye see in them? Thankfully, I come up with a last-minute excuse to leave.

When Skye and I hang out now, she'll say, "Let's smoke a joint."

The first time, I'd responded, "Only if we can get our hands on some parsley! I like the good stuff!"

We had a good laugh over that one.

But she keeps saying it. I find myself running out of excuses. I don't like smoking pot. I don't like the way it makes me feel. All spaced-out.

We got into a disagreement over smoking up recently. I asked her if she thought seeing this guy was a good idea. She responded, "This guy? You mean my boyfriend? The one I'm living with?" Then added, "Why are you making such a big deal about this, Morgan? Are we supposed to be like you and Nate? Practically a married couple, cooking and watching old movies together?"

MUSIC TRIVIA

My dad and I used to enjoy sharing bits of music trivia. And we'd make up random music games, like when a hit song came on the radio but you didn't immediately know the band's name, he'd say, "Name this band!"

"Genesis," I'd blurt out.

"Nope, you get two more tries."

Now Nate and I play music trivia. But it's much more intense, like music or history lessons. He goes on and on about new wave, post-punk, synth-pop, and dub. I have no idea what any of it means. And his dream is to go to CBGB, an iconic venue in New York City that he says is the birthplace of punk.

We're driving downtown and "Beds Are Burning" by Midnight Oil comes on the radio. Of course, Nate starts in. "This song's about giving land back to the Natives in Australia."

"I love the scene with Aboriginals in the video, but I guess I never thought about the meaning of the song," I reply.

"Listen to the words. They're a subversive group. They're trying to tell people there's more to the outback than Mick Dundee."

I chuckle. "I loved *Crocodile Dundee*!" And then, I consider his words further, "*You* should be selecting the songs for social studies assignments!"

Nate smiles shyly. You can tell he's flattered.

GO GET HER!

I'm at a house party with Nate. It's packed. It's been a while since I've been out. Skye's sister starts walking toward us, looking all intense like she's mad or something. She stops, smiles. "Hey, Morgan, Nate."

Phew. Skye's sister Cheryl is a force to be reckoned with. You don't want to be on her bad side. She sits down on the arm of the couch beside me and asks, "Have you seen Skye lately?"

"I haven't," I reply, immediately feeling guilty. Skye and I haven't spoken since our disagreement a couple of weeks ago.

"Troy is a total asshole," she says. "I've been hearing shit about him."

I nod, letting her know I'm listening, and that I agree with her.

She leans toward me and whispers, "Let's go get her."

"Now?" I ask. "It's one o'clock in the morning."

"Yes, now!" She's already standing. She grabs my hand and pulls me up.

"I'll be right back. Cheryl wants to talk to me about something," I say to Nate.

Cheryl and I shimmy through the crowded living room; she's holding my hand like a mother dragging a child. Once outside, I loosen my hand from her grip and we make our way to her car.

She gives me an update as we drive. Her old beater feels like a tin can. Cheryl says she'd tried to pick Skye up once, but she wouldn't leave with her. "So, you'll go this time," Cheryl says.

"What makes you think she'll listen to me?"

"You guys are best friends! Skye loves you."

I see lights on and people inside as we pull up to the house. Cheryl stops her car in the middle of the road and puts it into park. I look at her.

"Go get her!" she says impatiently.

I stumble, trying to hurry from the car, and then stand staring back at her.

The look on her face and her hand motion are saying *shoo* before she finally verbalizes, "Well, go!"

I close the door and she drives off. I watch her taillights disappear. It's the middle of the night, and I'm standing outside of a drug dealer's home. Friendship with Skye is challenging.

CHECKED OUT

My phone rings first thing in the morning. I was in a deep sleep; I can hardly move to answer it. I glance at the clock — it's 8 a.m. sharp. It's probably Nate, wondering where I went last night. When I reach for the phone, the cord gets tangled. I give it a yank. "Hello?" My voice is hoarse.

"Morgan! What happened to you?" He almost sounds angry.

"Good morning to you, too."

"Why did you take off? I was so worried about you."

"Cheryl took me to see Skye," I grumble. "More like, dumped me off there!"

"I would have gone with you. Why didn't you tell me?"

I told him Skye was high when I arrived and didn't say much. And that she looked thinner. Harder. "It was upsetting seeing her like that."

"She's getting mixed up with the wrong crowd."

"I didn't stay long. When I made for the door, Skye sarcastically remarked, 'Thanks for gracing us with your presence, Morgan.'"

"I'm sorry you had to see that. But you shouldn't have gone there alone." Nate sighs.

After hanging up, I stay in bed for a bit. It was a confusing night. Cheryl dragging me out of a party and dropping me off. I understand why she did it. She wants Skye away from that scene. We all do.

Whenever Skye and I hang out, it's never boring. We're usually laughing and having a good time. Even doing mundane things. And we never run out of things to talk about. Which is why it's hard to understand Skye's choice of a serious, live-in boyfriend. *Troy?* Not to mention how quickly this relationship has changed her.

TRIGGERED

I've heard things are getting worse between Skye and Troy. And with the drugs. Cheryl and I made another attempt to see Skye. I made sure she came with me this time — I wasn't going to let her dump me off again. But it was no use. Skye wouldn't even come to the door. It's a helpless feeling, seeing someone you love going down the wrong path.

A few weeks later, Cheryl calls and says my mother visited Skye, and that Skye seems to have responded to her. She's talking fast, so I concentrate to follow along. "From your mom's experience working with women at the Lodge, she believes Skye's been triggered from opening up about the abuse."

I stay silent, thinking back to when Skye and I got drunk and she told me about meeting my mom.

"Skye has never talked about being abused," Cheryl says. "Not even to me. We all knew it happened, but no one talks about that kind of stuff. And the creep who did it went to one of those schools. Your mom said he was likely abused there himself."

Her tone quickly shifts, sounding hopeful. "Your mom took Skye to the West End for lunch."

I can sense the love and concern Cheryl has for her sister. I can't imagine how hard this must be for her. It's been hard on me. I feel like I've lost my friend. I don't know how I would have handled things without Nate, especially after losing my father.

I'm glad Skye is getting help, but it's surreal that it's from my mom. And that she's suddenly in the picture — back in the picture.

CELEBRATION

Nate and I pass our final exams. We've completed eleventh grade! I score high in English Literature. Reading all those Jackie Collins novels paid off, after all! Bryan even jokes, "Do we have a writer in our midst? The next Jackie Collins!" I smile and stand a little straighter. *The NDN Jackie Collins.* It has a certain ring to it. Maybe without the smut. *Yes, no rez smut!* I have been writing more lately. Maybe it's something worth pursuing.

It feels like the end of an era — a beloved Alternate School era. Bryan was right about Alternate School being supportive. I never would have stayed in school if I hadn't gone there. Except it only goes to eleventh grade, so this means we're off to PRSS in September.

To celebrate, Nate takes us to Rodhos steakhouse. Then tells me — *he bought us tickets to Depeche Mode!* Their concert is in Vancouver! My first thought was, *I've never been to a concert before.* And then, *Depeche Mode? Are we white?* But then I remember I am obsessed with one of their hit songs. Nate said he's already asked my grandparents' permission, and that he's booked our plane tickets. The concert is in one week! I quickly let him know I'll pay my portion. He says, "It's a gift. I make enough money in one set of fishing to pay for the entire trip." He talks just like my dad.

"I love the song 'Personal Jesus,'" I share excitedly.

"Yeah, it's a mainstream hit," he replies.

The way he said "mainstream" makes me feel basic.

Then says, "'Policy of Truth' is my favorite."

I've never heard of it.

FIRST CONCERT AND OTHER FIRSTS

We check in at the Chateau Granville. I'm familiar with the area — I've stayed at the hotel with my dad many times. Nana and Grandpa prefer to stay on Robson. They say Granville is too seedy. Which it is. All the peep shows, sex stores, and pawn shops lining the street. Nate says he likes staying here for the location — it's easy to get everywhere on foot.

We go shopping at Pacific Centre almost as soon as we arrive. Man, can Nate shop! And such expensive clothing, too. *Harry Rosen?* He keeps offering to buy me stuff, but I have more than enough money. My grandparents made sure of that. I enjoy browsing. I don't make decisions as quickly. I haven't visited Vancouver in a while. It's a refreshing, welcoming change from Reitman's. We make our way in and out of familiar stores, and I eventually find a pair of faded Levi's 501s and a black cropped ribbed shirt for tonight's concert. I also buy sterling silver hoop earrings from a vendor on Granville Street. Nate says he'd planned to take me to Tsunami Sushi for dinner, but we run out of time. We end up grabbing New York Fries at the food court. He says we can go for sushi tomorrow.

On the way back to the hotel, Nate asks some guy on Granville to "run" for him. He gives him money for beer and coolers and says to keep the change.

We walk past the Nelson Hotel. My dad used to go to a dive bar on the main floor when we were in town. *I'll bump into fishermen there!* he'd say. I quickly dismiss the memory. Push it away with a blink.

Our shopping bags are scattered about our room. We have to look through so many bags searching for what we'll wear tonight. Nate heads to the shower. I lay my clothes out and reach for a chocolate hedgehog from Purdys. It's my first time vacationing without my family. I feel so grown up. I shiver with excitement.

Dread immediately sets in. I look over at the queen-sized bed. Nate hasn't been pressuring me for sex or anything, but now, here, how could we not? It's all I've been able to think about since Nate told me about the trip. I wish I could have talked to Skye about it. She would have prepared me. The only thing I thought to do was buy a new lace bra and underwear.

The concert is at the Pacific Coliseum in East Vancouver. We have to take a cab as we are running late.

I like the way Nate takes the lead in things. And how he holds my hand tight as we walk. It makes me feel safe.

I didn't know who the warm-up band was, but they are over by the time we get to our floor seats. *There are so many people!* The Coliseum is filled to the rafters. When Depeche Mode comes out, the crowd goes wild. I don't know most songs, but the energy is exhilarating.

The smell of weed is everywhere. A guy in front of us turns around and hands Nate a joint. He takes it, has a couple of puffs, and passes it back. It surprises me, but at the same time, why wouldn't he? It's all around us.

When "Personal Jesus" finally comes on, the entire stadium goes nuts — including Nate and me!

We buy matching concert T-shirts. And bump into a bunch of white people from Rupert. I don't know them, but Nate chats with them for a bit.

We have a few more drinks when we return to the room — actually, I have more than I should have. But I feel nervous. I've never had sex before.

We move to the bed. Nate reaches to turn the lamp off. City lights peek through the sheer curtains, but the room is mostly dark. He starts taking my clothes off. I expected to feel shy, but I don't. Maybe because of the way he's touching me. Slowly. Taking his time. He stares at my shoulders, gently kisses them. It makes me feel beautiful, loved, and warm down to my toes. Nate knows what he is doing, but it is still awkward to get in. *And it hurts!* As does the second time. And the time after that.

By the end of our trip, we are a couple of pros. I don't want our headboard-rattling sessions to end. I love the feeling of being that close to him. *How much closer to another human can you get?* And he's always super cuddly afterwards.

A BEAUTIFUL RUIN

A weekend away with your boyfriend should be on everyone's wish list. I haven't stopped smiling since we got back. It was uncomfortable having dinner with my grandparents last night. I felt like they could totally tell. I was radiating light like a damn Glo Worm — grin and all.

I want to tell Skye about our trip to Vancouver. I tried calling her boyfriend's place, but there was no answer. I've been thinking about her a lot lately. We've had our ups and downs, yes, but the good times definitely outweigh the bad. Besides, she hasn't had the easiest life.

I can't imagine how hard not living with her own family must be. We've never talked about it before. But, to not have a home to go to at the end of the day. Your own room to *just be*. Close your door and turn on some music.

It's no wonder she turned into a kleptomaniac. I'm not even exaggerating — she'd steal a stethoscope from a doctor if he wasn't looking. Then she'd turn around and give it to some kid like it's a toy. She's a klepto yes, but a generous one.

And the way she lives on Ichiban noodles? She eats a pack a day! Yet somehow, she stays so slim. And her skin is flawless — not a blemish on it. I teased her by saying I would get her a case of Sapporo Ichiban noodles for Christmas, and I'd wrap it and put a big ribbon on it.

Skye pays little regard to what the world says is acceptable. The so-called norm. And it's no wonder, with the cards she's been dealt.

She's not living in abject poverty or anything, but she's definitely lacking. And not just materially. She doesn't read or listen to music; she falls asleep if you put on a movie; and she chain-smokes cigarettes.

Lucky for her, booze isn't her vice. She knows her limit. It's men. Men are her vice. And she's merciless. Disposes of them like used Kleenex. And lately, I've heard she's getting into experimenting with drugs. Most recently, acid. Her sister is worried sick.

Yet Skye isn't someone you'd immediately pity. There's nothing woebegone about her. She's beautiful. Society makes allowances for people who look like her.

One time, when she had done some rotten thing or another, I said to her, "You're not a good person, Skye." I looked her right in the eye when I said it, then added, "I love you, but I sure don't like you." We were drinking. She started crying, then said, "That's the nicest thing anyone's ever said to me. I know I'm awful. But you're the only one who ever calls me out."

Nate says Skye has a willful spirit. Then adds, "Society punishes people like that."

Despite her willful ways, Skye is more than the sum of her parts. She gives so much of herself to the people she loves. Her family especially. She's clever, funny, and has an infectious laugh. People want to be around Skye. She's like a beautiful ruin. A ruin I am really starting to miss.

IT LOOKS GOOD ON YOU

Skye unexpectedly calls me! We haven't spoken in months. She must have picked up on my smoke signals. She invites me to New Moon for a chow mein bun. She is all casual on the phone, like nothing's happened. Like no time has elapsed. "See you there!" she says and hangs up.

When I arrive, she is already sitting in a booth. She looks good, back to herself.

"Hey," I say as I slide into the seat across from her.

She gives me a big smile. "I already ordered for us. I hope that's okay?"

"Yes! I'm starving."

Skye starts chatting immediately. She's in a good mood. She says she came from helping her gran with sewing. They are working on regalia. She says hand-sewing all those intricate little buttons is a lot of work — and her gran's eyes aren't good anymore.

Her family belongs to one of the Native dance groups in town. Their group was invited to perform during Expo 86. I didn't know Skye then, but she told me about it. It was the only time she'd ever been to Vancouver. Without skipping a beat, she tells me she's been helping her sister pack. Cheryl's being evicted. She ends by saying, "I'm relieved to be away from that total loser." I don't reply to that statement. I've learned my lesson.

When our food arrives, Skye removes the top bun and sprinkles soya sauce onto her chow mein. Still chatting, fork almost to her mouth, she stops. "You've had sex." Staring me in the face, she adds, "Oh my god, *Morgan Fairchild has had sex*."

Morgan Fairchild is one of her nicknames for me. I have barely said two words since sitting down. How could she possibly know? My face instantly flushes — I'm sure it's as red as the ketchup bottle on the table.

"You totally did!" She puts her fork down and holds her hand up to high-five me. High-fiving across the table makes me feel ridiculous. It's like I'm saying, *Yeah, man, I totally did. Put 'er there!*

"Tell me all the juicy details!" she says excitedly.

"Skye! I am not talking about it here. Lower your voice." I look around the dimly lit restaurant.

"It looks good on you." She can't help herself. "I'm so happy for you."

She's still smiling, "Tell me later?"

"I will. I will." I chuckle.

It feels good being together again. I tell her about Depeche Mode, and she tells me she's feeling single and ready to mingle. It feels like nothing has changed, and yet everything has.

She doesn't mention my mom, which, surprisingly, disappoints me. I wanted an update but couldn't bring myself to ask.

YOU'RE NOT DRINKING

Cheryl's having an eviction party. Skye insists I go. I'm not in the mood but want to spend time with her. Besides, Nate's fishing. What else is there to do on a Friday night? We pick up a bottle of Malibu and pineapple juice for a mix.

The party is in full swing when we arrive, even though the house is empty of furniture. A ghetto blaster sits on top of the fridge. Trooper's "3 Dressed Up as a 9" is playing. We manage to find two mismatched mugs in the cupboard and mix our drinks, cheers each other, and take a sip. Skye starts grading girls' outfits. She mostly gives out threes. She's ruthless and is making up her own lyrics. After a girl walks past us, she says, "Three dressed up as a three."

"Skye! I'd hate to walk past you if we weren't friends!" I exclaim.

"You're an eleven dressed as a seven, baby!" Then adds, "Because you're always hiding under baggy sweatshirts!"

The living room is crowded with mainly older guys. They say things like "Whose own, are you?" when we walk past.

"Eee, sick! We're cousins," Skye replies over her shoulder.

It's entertaining watching her interact with people. She's likeable and funny. Friendly to everyone, whether they're "cool" or not. It's probably her best quality.

We circle the living room and dining room, and head back to the kitchen, making small talk with people along the way.

"Should we have another drink?" Skye asks as she places her empty mug on the counter, then looks at mine. It's still full. "Why aren't you drinking?"

"I'm not feelin' it," I reply casually.

"What do you mean, *not feeling it*?" She fixes her gaze on mine. "Morgan, not in the mood to drink. That's not like you."

Not long ago, I'd get stupid drunk on weekends. Skye and I would spend Sundays piecing together events. Laughing at all the dumb things I did. Like the time she said I climbed from the back seat to the front of a cab; she said I was practically nuzzling the back of the taxi driver's neck.

Then I heard the expression "sloppy drunk." *Sloppy drunk*. It sounded pitiful and weak. I felt instant shame. And an awareness, for the first time, of what I didn't want to be. And then I met Nate. I never wanted him to see me like that. Other than the night of the concert, I barely drank anymore.

"I'm not feeling well." I look down at the mug in hand. "The smell of pineapple juice is making me nauseous."

"*Oh, my god*. Are you pre—"

"Skye! Of course not. And lower your damn voice! Sheesh, go starting "Rupert rumours," I snap.

"Well, what the hell. How long have you *not been feeling well*?" Her right hand is resting on the Malibu bottle, her eyes on me.

"It started this past week."

"Are you late for your period?"

"I don't track that closely. But my last was before Vancouver, and that was well over a month ago . . ."

Skye tears her eyes from me and turns to make a drink, "We better go to the Green Clinic on Monday."

MONDAY MORNING

I don't feel well, but I don't think I am pregnant. After all, we use condoms. So when the doctor gives me the results, I can hardly believe it.

"The test is positive. You are pregnant," he says.

"Yeah, right," I respond. But when I look over at Skye's face, the nurse's, and then back to the doctor, it hits me.

I don't remember much else that is said, something about a list of options to consider. I am just thankful Skye came with me. Leaving the clinic, she stops, her voice full of concern, and says, "You can't handle an abortion, Morgan. You're not strong enough."

"What's that supposed to mean?" I ask.

"You know that abortion sign on the highway outside of Terrace, with a picture of a fetus in the mother's womb?"

I nod, to let her know I'm following.

"It says, 'Abortion — they're forgetting someone...'"

I nod again.

"It hits you in the gut every time you pass it . . ." She looks away. "And every year after, you're fully aware how old it would have been."

I stop walking. "Skye, how come you've never told me this before?"

"It's not something you go around openly sharing, Morgan. It's painful."

"I feel lightheaded," I say, as we continue making our way to my truck.

"Here, let me drive," Skye says, taking my keys and helping me climb in.

BY THE WAY...

Prince Rupert gets so much rain that when we finally get sun, it's almost magical — a damn miracle. Everyone walks around downtown and at the waterfront. Patios at the Crest or Breakers fill up, with people looking to soak up the sun. Fishing closed today. Nate says he'll come over when he is done on the boat. He likes to stay on top of repairs so the boat is ready for the next opening. He doesn't like to put things off.

I grab a few things at the mall before heading home. I've had the whole week to process the *news*. I still don't know how to feel. How I'm supposed to feel. I've been fretting over how I'll break it to Nate. The wording never sounds right in my head. Do I tell him right away or after we settle in? Do I lead up to it or blurt it out? And I can't seem to shake feeling guilty. Like it's my fault. Why hadn't

I thought about birth control pills? Ever. Is that something my mother would have recommended? Dad certainly never brought it up.

It's Friday. My grandparents have gone out for dinner, and then they're going to the pub afterwards — their usual routine. I'm relieved we will have privacy. Just in case Nate loses it when I tell him I'm pregnant and breaks up with me.

Nate walks through the door, looking tanned, handsome, and happy. He pulls me into a tight embrace, then pushes me away and says, "Let me look at you!" He lets out a sigh and kisses me. We start kissing with heated intensity, like saving lives is involved. He lifts my shirt over my head and reaches for my breast. All of a sudden, we're going at each other, removing the rest of our clothes. I quickly forget the important news I wanted to share.

I lie back afterwards, done, gladly spent. Nate falls to the bed, panting. "That was good," he manages.

"You need a cigarette?" I joke.

He chuckles and leans to kiss my shoulder, then sits up. "We should order pizza. I'm starved."

"Sure," I reply. As I lean to reach for my clothes, a feeling of dread washes over me. When do I tell him? How do I tell him? By the way . . .

"I'm pregnant." The words just come out.

Nate has his back to me. He turns slowly. "What did you say?"

I can't repeat it. I move to lie back down and pull the sheet over my head.

The room goes silent.

The silence lasts longer than feels comfortable. Bearable.

Nate lies back down, but still says nothing. I bite my lip to keep from crying. He moves onto his side and rests on an elbow facing me and pulls the sheet from my face. He caresses my cheek with his finger, then moves my hair away. "When did you find out?"

"On Monday."

He kisses my forehead gently, slips an arm under me, and pulls me close. "You okay?"

I shrug.

"Have you thought about what you want to do?"

I know what I want to do, but I'm afraid to say it. What if it's the opposite of what he wants? A tear rolls down my face.

"Hey." He looks at me. "I love you. I'll have this baby with you. Or I'll support whatever you want."

I wasn't expecting the tears. They keep falling.

"Can I say something else?" he adds.

I nod.

"If I had it my way, we'd have this baby. That's my say."

I can hardly get the words out. "It's what I want, too."

BREAKING THE NEWS

I like to think we are "sharing the news," but that isn't how things feel. Skye is happy when I say we are keeping the baby. Even my grandparents are. Well, maybe not *happy*, but supportive. Nan gets teary-eyed and talks about my dad. He's been on my mind a lot lately, too. How would he have reacted? Even my mother crossed my mind. Grandpa asks if we are getting married and says it should be before the baby comes. *Married?* That is the furthest thing from my mind. I tell my grandparents on my own. Nate tried insisting we do it together, but I couldn't. I knew they wouldn't freak out or anything, but I still wanted that time alone with them.

Nate shares the news with his parents on his own, too — *I didn't want any part of that*. I haven't even met them yet! Good grief. What kind of impression am I going to make now?

It's the weekend, and we are going for lunch with Nate's parents. We're meeting at Smiles Café. I make sure to eat crackers before we go to keep my nausea under control.

Lunch is so awkward. Torture, actually. I don't know how I'm going to get my food down, let alone keep it down. Nate's dad seems nice enough, and he's trying to be friendly, but his mom? She's a piece of work. When they first sit down, she stares across the table at me like I am some hussy, a two-bit nothing who trapped her son. Shame wells inside me — it's a familiar feeling. The only thing she asks me is, "Are you planning on continuing with school?"

And don't get me started on Nate. It's like he's completely checked out. He's here, but he isn't. I want to kick him under the table. At least our food comes quickly.

"My favorite fish-and-chips in town," Nate's dad says.

"Yup," Nate agrees.

I stir my clam chowder with my spoon. Trying to cool it down, but also, I can't bring myself to eat it. I feel like I'm going to puke. No one says much else. "Mmm," here and there. Or, "Can we get more tartar sauce?"

Then Nate's mom says, "It's not going to be easy. It's a big responsibility."

"And we would know," his dad quickly adds. "Your mom was your age when she had your sister."

His mom gives his dad a good glare over that one. The table goes back to silence. Thankfully, no one is interested in lingering. His dad asks for and pays the bill. And says, "You kids take care" as he slides out of the booth.

We make our way home. I'm so angry — seething. I'm trying to wrap my mind around what happened. Why did my smart, confident boyfriend just sit there? Bent over his plate like an empty shell of a person, just shoveling food into his mouth? We pull up to my place, and Nate turns the car off.

"What was that?" I ask.

"What do you mean?"

"You sat there and said nothing! It was so uncomfortable."

"I know my mom's difficult."

"I can handle *difficult*. But you checking out like that was worse."

"I'm sorry. But this is stressful. You thought that was bad? You should have heard her reaction when I told her. She really tore a strip off of me."

He looks like a lost little boy.

CONCERNED, MY ASS

Skye comes to visit. I haven't felt like doing much of anything lately, with feeling so nauseous all the time. I am glad she's okay with sitting around and hanging out.

"I bumped into Bryan uptown," I tell her. "I asked if Alternate had any options for pregnant teens."

"What did he say?" Skye's on her tummy, flipping through a magazine.

"You wouldn't believe his response," I reply.

Skye looks up from the magazine.

"He said: 'If you don't have an abortion, you'll spend the rest of your life in poverty and you'll never be a writer.'"

"That asshole said that? He has no right, Morgan."

"He wasn't *mean*. . . . He seemed more . . . concerned."

"Concerned, my ass," she sneers.

"Skye." I laugh. "Bryan's been nothing but good to me."

"And a writer? What's that supposed to mean?"

"I've been writing more these days. You remember reading some of my stories."

She nods.

"I got a high mark on my English final."

"That's cool." She goes quiet, then asks, "How does Nate feel about the pregnancy?"

"He was the first to say he wanted to keep the baby."

"He better have — he'd have to deal with *me* if he didn't!" She holds a clenched fist up as she says it.

"He's just glad we no longer need condoms. And he wants to do it *all the time* now!"

Skye bursts out laughing.

"Seriously, why does anyone need it so many times a day?" I add.

Skye's almost crying from laughter. "Oh, Morgan," she manages. "You crack me up."

WWJD?

I open my nightstand drawer and see a copy of *Chances*, and I suddenly realize I haven't read in months. *Months?* How is that possible? I stare at the bubblegum-pink cover with seafoam-green writing. Once an all-time favorite. I'd lose myself in the pages. Lifestyles of the rich and famous — lunch at Chateau Marmont, the Ivy, Spago, or the Polo Lounge. Why haven't I been reading? Because I was grieving my father? Too busy falling in love? Getting pregnant? Or was I ashamed after Nate made fun of Jackie Collins's books? I pick up the pocket-sized book and leaf through the pages. Or maybe because her books are trash. Smut, as Skye had said. They definitely don't deal with real-life issues. Not like the books Nate reads. Malcom X, Gandhi.

What would Jackie do? Jackie couldn't help me with shit. Like, how do I get over losing my father? Should I talk to my mother again? I'm seventeen and having a baby, any suggestions on motherhood? Jackie Collins, once my ticket out of Prince Rupert, is suddenly no help. *Of no consequence.* Sounds like some lame line she'd write.

I toss the book into the drawer and slam it shut.

MORNING SICKNESS

Nate's been fishing so much this summer. I almost prefer him not being around. I feel so nauseous all the time, I'd rather be alone. The other day, I ate an orange for breakfast, drove uptown, parked, and opened my truck door just in time for projectile vomit to fly out of my mouth. I've also started feeling anxious. When Nate leaves for fishing, dread washes over me. I worry his boat is going to sink. And I can't shake the feeling. Nana had to lie me down on the couch one day. She put a cold cloth on my head. I didn't share my irrational thoughts with her. She just thought it was morning sickness.

When fishing is closed, Nate comes back excited and energized. He reminds me of my dad. They both love (loved) fishing. There's nothing else they would rather do. Even when it's rough fishing, it's like a high for them. The adrenaline-rush of Man vs. the Ocean. And, of course, there's the money.

Nate's always in a good mood when he's done. Seeing his smiling face brings some relief. But I feel bad that I can't match his energy and enthusiasm. After a few days together, I can tell he gets restless. He suddenly has work he needs to do on the boat.

ALASKA MEN

Skye has met someone new. He's a Native fisherman from Metlakatla, Alaska. He's also a crabber. "He's loaded!" she gushes to me.

"Alaska! Have you been watching too much Oprah? Is he looking for a wife?" I ask, all smart-alecky.

Skye must have seen the episode about the Alaska bachelors and the shortage of women there, because she throws her head back in laughter. "Maybe." She smiles coyly. Then says, "He treats me good, and he's so generous. He even has a credit card!"

It's nice to see her happy. She deserves to be spoiled.

She's been seeing him for a few weeks now. "I'm completely gaga. *For real this time!*" she says giddily.

I can't help but smile. She's full-on blissed out.

Then, quickly shifting tone, she says, "Speaking of Oprah. I have been watching her shows. She talks about the same kind of stuff your mom does. Your mom's pretty smart, Morg."

"You still see her?" I ask, trying to sound casual.

"We've met a few times. She's helped me so much."

A few times? "What, are you guys best friends now?"

"Get this. Your mom says I'm a natural leader!" She holds her head high and chuckles. "And that I can help our people."

"Of course you are, Skye. And people really like you."

She smiles, but the shine in her eyes quickly fades. Like she doesn't believe it. "Back to my guy!" She grins. "His name is Shaun. I want you to meet him."

SKYE'S MAN

Skye and her new man invite Nate and me for Chinese at Galaxy Gardens. Of course, the guys get right into talking about fishing! Meanwhile, I focus on studying Shaun. I try to read his body language. Looking for any warning signs. Hoping he's nothing like the last guy. You can tell he's a high roller right off the bat. He's wearing a gold hayetsk pendant. It's rare to see copper shield designs worn as pendants. They are a symbol of wealth and status.

As we reach for our menus, Shaun says, "Order whatever you want, guys. I'm buying." He starts us off with two orders of lettuce wraps. Skye is nineteen now, and Shaun is a few years older than her, so they order beers as well. Nate and I sit like a couple of punks. Well, Nate does; I wouldn't be drinking either way.

Shaun doesn't seem that bright or funny — two key traits for me. Right up there with looks. But he's friendly, generous, and good to Skye. He's openly affectionate and refers to her as "babe." She's beaming, really radiating, which is nice to see.

We all enjoyed ourselves at dinner and promised to do it again. Unfortunately, Shaun's only in town for a few more weeks.

HELP?

It's back-to-school time. Nate is officially attending senior high. Twelfth grade. I couldn't do it. I couldn't imagine walking around with a pregnant teen belly like Spike from *Degrassi*. Nate says I shouldn't feel too bad, that I can always do my GED later.

Nate's unofficially living with us. I didn't ask my grandparents if he could move in. It happened gradually. They don't seem to mind. Grandpa's just grateful to have help around the house. Nate still needs to move the rest of his stuff over. It kind of feels like we're in transition — in limbo.

We haven't discussed plans for when the baby arrives yet. Will we stay with my grandparents? Or find our own place?

Skye comes over to visit this afternoon. She says she told my mom about the baby. I don't respond, although my mom has been on my mind more and more lately. I found the framed picture of her that my dad kept on his dresser when I was going through an old box. It was weird staring at her photo. We look so much alike, yet she's a stranger to me. Nan's been hinting around about her, too. She told me she bumped into her uptown.

"She said congratulations." Skye continues, "And wants to know if she can help."

"*Help?* With what, mothering advice? Hah."

Skye stares at me. And for the first time, says nothing.

STATISTIC

I'm sitting in the waiting area at the dentist's office, leafing through an outdated magazine. I'm five months and showing. Family and friends are constantly rubbing my belly. I'm still not used to it. Except when Nate rubs it, of course. He started loving-up my belly early on. He'll talk to it and say, "Hey in there, I'm your father." It's adorable.

A white girl enters, checks in, and sits down. I don't look up. I don't want to make eye contact, which will lead to conversation. It's the introverted only-child in me. I recognize her from my junior high days, but can't remember her name. She hung out with the popular girls. I glance at the stomach I can no longer hide. It hits me every once in a while — what have I done?

I had hopes and dreams of leaving Rupert. Of travel. Of maybe even being a writer.

I'm glad I've fixed myself up a bit today. I found a woven sisal bag in the basement. (It's like the one Annie wore in *Annie Hall*.) Nana said it was hers from the seventies. Her hippie days, she'd boasted. I'm wearing black maternity leggings, a white Club Monaco sweatshirt, and gold hoop earrings. The colorful woven texture of the bag brings the otherwise basic outfit together.

The girl reaches for a magazine on the square coffee table. "Slim pickings, huh?" she says.

I look up from my magazine and smile. "Yeah." Hoping that's the end of our small talk.

"Congratulations."

I look over at her. She's touching her tummy, smiling at me. "When are you due?" she asks.

My face flushes. Like shame's been injected directly into my veins. Yet another pregnant teen. A statistic. "I'm five months. Four more to go." I manage a smile. I look back at the magazine, trying to seem immersed in it.

"I think you're brave."

White girl can't read the room. I look over at her.

"I know girls from school who had abortions. Even some of my friends." She whispers the last part.

Just then, the receptionist calls my name. I nod at the girl. Not sure if I am nodding at what she'd said or saying bye.

As the hygienist cleans my teeth, I think about her words — that girls from school had had abortions. So I'm not the only teen who's gotten herself pregnant. White girls get pregnant, too.

But we choose to keep our babies — that's the only difference.

The shameful stigma lessens somewhat, even if it's only an inner sense. The world would continue to see what the world would see. A statistic.

BABY NAMES

My life felt stagnant before I met Nate. Stuck. On hold, but I didn't know what for. I felt like he plucked me from the dreary mundaneness of "Rupert life."

Nate's not waiting around for "one day." He *lives* life. The here and now. After my father died, Nate's love felt like a healing salve to my grieving heart. Something stronger than Devil's club. *How could I be so lucky?*

It makes me sad that my dad never got to know Nate. I'm sure he would have liked him. Of course he would have. *What about that Jones boy?* he'd said that one time.

Nate and I have been focusing mainly on boys' names. For some reason, I'm convinced the baby will be a boy. Nate starts reading out unique names from movie credits. We throw around other ideas: musicians' names, famous actors. None that stick. Or are "worthy," Nate says. One day he says, "If it's a boy, we should name him after your dad."

I'd thought of it myself, and Nana had mentioned it, too. But hearing it now stirs deep emotions within me. I start to cry. (I've been doing a lot of that lately.) Nate attempts to pull me into an embrace, but we're not able to reach each other. We stand awkwardly, my belly between us.

Along with my newfound tears, I've also been struggling with feelings of jealousy. When I see men my father's age. Or when Nate speaks about his father. It hits me in the gut. Like a punch. Nate helps his dad on the boat, goes to Terrace with him for parts, or for lunch at West End. Like my dad and I did. I try to dismiss my feelings. Tell myself that I'm being unreasonable. *But it hurts.*

It's not that I want anyone else to suffer, but *why*? Why did my father have to pass away so young? And so suddenly. Such a beautiful life, lost. Gone.

"Little James," I manage and smile.

Nate smooths my hair near my face. "James Jones," he says, and kisses my forehead. "It's a good name."

MEYER LANSKY

Nate is always two steps ahead of everyone. The wheels turn as he maps out next moves or anticipates what may go wrong. It's not just street smarts. There's more to it. It's like he's playing a game of chess. His moves are calculated. He's perceptive and quick. He sees things and people almost in an instant. Even in a movie, he'll know what scene is coming. And nine times out of ten, he's right! When I question him about it, he brushes it off and says it's common sense.

And he knows *everyone* in town. He says hello to every other person we pass. Natives from different reserves, people financially well-off or not. He knows the details and histories of families, parents, and grandparents.

"How do you know these things?" I ask him.

"You have to. It's important."

I stare at him, still not understanding.

"This is our community. Our people. You should know where people are from," he adds.

My family tends to keep to themselves. Well, Dad had his fishing and drinking buddies. They were mostly Natives. But he didn't track things as closely as Nate does. Wasn't as involved. And maybe because Nana married a white man, she's not as connected to the community.

Nate has a lot of friends, too: buddies from fishing; white guys he plays basketball with; Native guys he plays soccer with; kids from Alternate. Some good friends, some questionable. A few are downright shady. One of them gave Nate the nickname Meyer Lansky. I'm familiar with the name from my Jackie Collins novels. I laugh at that because I can see it. Nate misses nothing. Knows the comings and goings of the community. He could totally be a Meyer Lansky.

Flower Duty

At my medical appointment, they ask who my support team will be for the delivery room. Team? Other than Nate, I hadn't planned on a *crew* being there. Sheesh, it's kind of a private moment!

I don't know what to expect. According to the movies there will be a lot of screaming and a lot of pain. Like that isn't bad enough, I'm now approximately the size of a beached whale. My face is puffy, and I'm uncontrollably gassy.

"Not to worry, dear," Nana reassures me. "You're just retaining water."

I'm due any day now. Nana and I are watching one of her soap operas, where a woman has just given birth. Her hospital room is filled with balloons and flowers welcoming the bundle of joy into the world. "Nana," I say, pointing at the screen. "I want my hospital room to look like that."

Nana has already shared that she would probably faint if she came into the delivery room. As much as she would love to be there, she said she couldn't handle it. Suddenly, she flashes her cute little grin like it's game on.

"Now flower duty, I can definitely do, granddaughter!"

EL PREGO

I call Skye and ask her to come visit me. I tell her I am not getting out much these days, with being so impossibly large and all. She comes over right away.

"God! You're so dramatic! You made it sound like we needed to bring in a crane to move you," Skye says as she leans to give me a quick hug.

I have a good laugh over it. A much-needed belly laugh. She also has a new nickname for me — *El Prego*. Like I'm a tub of tomato sauce.

She's wearing a white T-shirt with a Native design of an eagle. Her family's crest. It must be new; I've never seen her wear it before. She also has a carved-gold Native pendant. A gift from her boyfriend — *a generous gift!* She's still beaming. Happiness looks good on her. Like it's long overdue. I'm happy for her, yet, at that exact moment, I find myself longing for the freedom she's emanating. She seems so carefree. I feel anything but. I feel like an albatross has been cast around my neck. I'm large and immobile. Not beautiful like Skye. And it suddenly hits me — *what have I gotten myself into?*

I'd felt the same when I met up with Jess for lunch at New Moon last week. She was visiting for the long weekend. I could tell she was disappointed in me. There was an awkwardness between us that wasn't there before. We suddenly had nothing in common. She talked about college, partying, and boys, and there I was, sitting with my enormous pregnant belly—a Laughing Buddha Belly. But I wasn't laughing. I could barely fake a smile. Jess proudly shared that she'd passed all her classes and had gotten a job serving at The Keg steakhouse. I had nothing cool or exciting to share. *I have newly discovered stretch marks!* Oh, and an aching back. And wait for it . . . never-ending gas problems!

"Earth to Morgan," Skye says.

My deep thoughts ran away on me. I blink, trying to brush them off.

"You aren't listening to me," Skye complains.

"Sorry, I'm just tired." I can tell my sudden mood change has sapped the energy from the room.

Skye abruptly rises and says, "I have to run. I just stopped by to say a quick hello."

"Hey, will you come into the delivery room?" I ask her.

"Hell yeah," she replies. "Even if you didn't ask me, I'd be there." She walks over and rubs my belly before she leaves, "My little El Prego."

LETTER NUMBER TWO

Three days have passed since my due date. Skye stops by for a visit, and Nan says I need to be out walking to encourage the baby to come out. Skye immediately stands up and offers to take me. "Come on, Momma. Let's go."

We make our way toward the end of the street. The sun is trying to make an appearance, but it's mainly overcast. "I saw your mom yesterday," Skye says.

"She's still in town?" I reply coolly.

"Yeah. She says I don't know how to *receive love*," Skye says with a snicker.

"Hmm..." I reply, not quite sure what that even means.

"She said most Natives don't. It's because we're '*oppressed* people,' and because of those damn residential schools." She pauses and then continues, "They destroyed our families and communities, Morgan. Cut us off at the knees."

I don't say anything.

"Look around us. Alcoholism, broken families, single mothers..."

I think back to my mom's letter. *I didn't feel worthy of your father's love.*

"This isn't how it's supposed to be, Morg. We're not inherently flawed or broken people. This was something *done to us.*"

There's something different in Skye's voice.

"Oh" — she stops and turns to me — "your mom wanted me to give you this letter."

I look sideways, not wanting Skye to read my reaction, and hold out my hand. I place the letter in my sweater pocket, and we continue walking.

What I really want to do is turn around, go home, and read it.

After Skye leaves, I head down to our bedroom and immediately open the letter. It talks about the baby coming and motherhood. She mentions seeing Nate and me in Zellers and says Nate looks like a kind, intelligent man who will be a wonderful father, as I will a mother. And what an exciting time it is for us. She said she grieved the grandfather my dad would have been. Then she talks about residential school. Says she can't openly share its impact on her. It's too painful. But she's been journaling about it. She says it's helping her process those experiences — not only hers but those of her parents and her brothers. And, of course, the greater Native community. She says she is trying to understand what happened to us, and how we got here. It's the same message Skye just shared — verbatim. I smile at that. I reread her words. Each time, they hit harder and harder. I think about Dad's framed picture of my beautiful mother. A big smile. Yet hiding so much pain. I feel a great sadness wash over me, but also a knowing. *It isn't us.* This was something *done to us*! I feel a heavy release. And for the first time, forgiveness.

WHITE MAN'S POTION

I think about my mom's letter for the next few days. Her life, her parents. I even think about people like Skye and the childhood she never had. That's loss. The world has been cruel. There's been so much suffering in our communities. So much hurt.

Uncle Stuart doesn't drink. He never has. He's a teetotaler. He calls alcohol "the white man's evil potion." And says it has been used as a weapon against us, introduced as an evil negotiating pawn. He says it was given to us like candy to a kid and then snatched away, made illegal: *You can't have that.*

He said in order to buy alcohol, an Indian would have to give up his Indian status card. He also says it's a legal form of poison. "It causes more harm than cigarettes and drugs combined. And not just for our people."

Uncle Stuart often says things like that. Since Grandpa is a) white and b) enjoys a fine whiskey, you can tell he doesn't like it. He never handles blame well. And this is probably why Nan doesn't have Uncle Stuart over for dinner as much as she should.

LITTLE BUNDLE

It's corny when you hear mothers gush about their babies. Their little bundle of joy is perfect; they fell instantly in love; their life is now complete . . . blah blah blah.

It's all true.

I fall instantly in love. Well, once the anesthetic wears off. I had to have a C-section. A cesarean.

Nate doesn't leave my side throughout, reassuring me along the way. I fall even more in love with him. I didn't think that was possible. And then seeing him with her! *Yes, her.*

When he places her next to me, I start to cry. Nate assumes something is wrong, but I tell him I am crying because I love her so much. He assures me he does, too. And Nana delivers on the flowers and balloons. My room is filled with "It's a girl!" and "Welcome!" balloons and flowers.

The few weeks after are a tireless blur. And utter bliss. She brings so much softness and joy. She takes to breastfeeding beautifully. At least that's what the nurse says. My body is sore. No one told me I'd tire so easily. Or that I'd undergone major surgery, and I should take it easy.

Nate takes naturally to fatherhood. He doesn't even mind poopy diaper duty. She sleeps pretty soundly, too, only wakes up once in the middle of the night for a feed. Surprisingly, motherhood feels natural to me, too. This little bundle is under my care, and I take that job seriously. And to heart. Things feel so different. I can't describe it. My world has changed.

Nate's parents were away when she was born, but they bought her a Peg Perego carriage stroller. It was almost *six hundred dollars*! It's deluxe, all right. Nan and Grandpa bought a car seat and a cozy sheepskin cushion. Of course, Skye already has a nickname for her, *the Royal Baby*.

She's two months old already. We have mostly been at home, adjusting to all the changes. But there's a feast happening this evening at the Fisherman's Hall. It's going to be her first outing. I make sure to put on her prettiest pink dress. I know the little floral headband won't stay on for long, but I put it on anyway. Nate and Nana gush and grab their cameras when I bring her upstairs. Seeing their love for her is so special. It warms my heart. It's hard to believe anyone can love her as much as me, but they do.

We find a table at the feast and settle in. There are a lot of people already, and the hall is nearly full. I lift the baby from her car seat and stand, holding her. Adjust her dress and little headband. She smirks in her sleep. Of course, I smile back at her. I look up and spot my mother and Skye and I slowly make my way to where they are standing. People smile as I pass, saying, "Look, a baby." I spot Nate at the back. He sees the direction I'm walking in and stares with a serious look, then nods reassuringly.

When I reached my mom and Skye, no one says a word. Which is unusual for Skye. It's like the room has gone silent, but it's not an uncomfortable silence. "Meet Miss Jaime Jones," I say. "Jaime Bea Jones. Jaime is after my father, and Bea after Nana."

My mom's eyes fill with tears. Happy tears.

I extend my arms toward her, for her to take the baby. As she does, she slowly whispers, "Hello, precious Jaime. A beautiful, fitting name."

— ONE YEAR LATER —

Nana and I are in the audience at the Chatham House. My mom is speaking about women's healing and we're waiting for her to take the stage.

My mom and I have taken things slowly in reconnecting. I needed to adapt to being a new mother and she was respectful of that. Offered to help out when needed, but gave us our space. Baby Jaime adores her Dzi'i. And rightfully so: My mom's a loving grandmother to her.

When Nana told me Mom had invited us to attend her presentation, I said yes right away. Nate is at home with the baby. I can't believe she's already a one-year-old. Sweet baby Jaime. It's good for him to spend time with her on his own. He's always fishing and misses so much of her growing. So many firsts. Nan tells me not to think like that. She says he's working hard to provide for us. We're still living with my grandparents, trying to save money, but I recently turned nineteen and my grandfather made the decision that we should move into my dad's house. "It's yours," Grandpa said. He's given the tenants notice and we're going to do minor renovations. Nate is going to do most of the work himself. Paint the entire inside and install new lighting fixtures.

Nate's parents offered financial support, but we don't see much of them. They're always traveling. And his sister is still attending university.

Skye should be here, I think to myself. She has a new boyfriend, again. He's worse than all the others combined. And she's getting back into drugs. I last spoke with her more than six months ago. It's so sad. She was so full of hope and optimism when she was dating the guy from Alaska. And getting together with my mother. I don't know what changed or what happened. I left a message with her sister about my mom's event, but I didn't hear back.

It's a full house. The program begins with opening remarks, then the MC introduces my mother. She strides across the stage to applause. I beam with pride and Nana reaches for my hand. My mom stands at the podium, readies herself, and begins speaking. Her voice is strong and steady, empowered. She talks a bit about herself and her background, and then about Indian residential schools. And Phil Fontaine, the National Chief of the Assembly of First Nations who bravely spoke up about abuses at those schools. She directly quotes him: "We had to confront this issue — as shameful, painful, and embarrassing as it was going to be. It was our responsibility to do so."

Nana lets out a sigh. A deep, weighty sigh.

My mom speaks to the collective trauma suffered as a result of those schools, the loss of language, culture, and teachings. And the abuse. There's a solemness to her tone, but also conviction. The audience is silent. Hanging on her every word. I side-eye Nana to see if she's all right; her eyes are fixed on my mom.

My mother shares that she's been journaling. Writing her feelings down. She says it's a beneficial way to get them out of her. Says she's held that sickness in her body for too long. She starts reading a piece from her journal:

What if you were torn from your loving home?
As young as four years old
Forced to live far away
In a cold and cruel institution.

Stark walls and stern faces watch over you.
You're told everything about you is wrong.
The color of your skin, your language, and your culture.

Strangers, so different from the ones you've known,
telling you: you are less than.
Looking you in the eye, saying again and again
you're good for nothing.

The audience is filled with mostly older Native people. I glance around to see their reactions. Some are looking down, others are nodding in agreement, and some are sitting with their arms tightly crossed.

You're fed bland, poor-quality food.
Even then, it's rationed.

Interactions with your siblings are forbidden.
If you see them suffering
There's nothing you can do.

You have to ignore feelings of sadness, pain, or anger
because you're punished if you cry or act out.

You have to numb your body and sense of personal space.
They are often violated.
Sometimes in the cruelest manner.

Anytime you see or experience human touch,
it's an act of abuse.

Children torn from our embraces
wasn't our first encounter with injustice. Or trauma.
Colonizers' lying, thieving, evil ways were widespread.
Stolen land and broken promises.

Men were left with feelings of powerlessness.
Women were silent. Overcome with grief.
In the deafening silence of an empty home,
they grew numb.

Some parents turned to self-medication.
Drowned their sorrows and shame in the bottle.

When children eventually returned home,
if they did at all, as some didn't survive,
there was a disconnect in the family, a breakdown.
They were like strangers.

Children returned home with wounds unseen.

And the vow of silence forced upon them.

Parents sat emotionless.

What could they say?

They'd been there themselves.

They knew what happened at those schools.

But their tongue, too, had been silenced.

Culture was no longer practiced in the community.

It had long since been banned as illegal.

There was no song, dance, or healing salve to save them.

Silence hung over homes, the community, as if in mourning.

A mourning that would last for generations.

The room was silent, and then slowly, broke into applause.

I WANT HER TO KNOW

An unexpected blessing from having my mother back in my life is hearing her tell stories about my dad. Ones I haven't heard before. Funny stories that have us both in tears from laughter.

She's even started talking about him to baby Jaime. I overhear her in her gentle, soothing voice, sharing special memories of him.

The dull ache of losing my father will always be there. But talking about him helps. I've started sharing stories with Jaime, too. Even if she doesn't understand yet. I want her to know. I want her to grow up hearing and knowing about my father. I tell her she's named after him — she's his blood. His most precious granddaughter.

I tell her how he was a great fisherman who told the best stories. He was funny and animated. The way he would exaggerate the size or catch of fish or how rough or high the waves were.

I tell her that he was a good dancer who happened to make the best pancakes.

And that he was a kind and loving father. The best father.

"What a combination," I tell baby Jaime.

"What a loss," I whisper.

When "We're Here for a Good Time" comes on the radio, I turn up the volume or scoop her up and dance with her in my arms and say, "This was your grandfather's favorite song."

AUTHOR'S NOTE

No one in my family attended Indian residential schools. I didn't take writing about this subject lightly. While this account is fiction, I aimed to tell our history with the utmost honor and respect to residential school survivors. I was careful in writing about sensitive subjects, but didn't water down the painful effects.